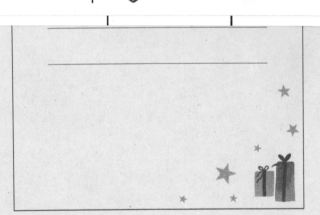

NOEL STREATFEILD was born in Sussex in 1895 and was one of three sisters. After working in munitions factories and canteens for the armed forces when the First World War broke out, Noel followed her dream of being on stage and went to RADA where she became a professional actress.

She began writing children's books in 1931 and *Ballet Shoes* was published in 1936. She quickly became one of the most popular authors of her day. When she visited Puffin exhibitions, there were queues right out of the building and all the way down the street. She was one of the first winners of the Carnegie Medal and was awarded an OBE in 1983.

Noel Streatfeild died in 1986.

Books by Noel Streatfeild

NOEL STREATFEILD

Christmas
with the
Chrystals
and other
stories

A PUFFIN BOOK

PUFFIN BOOKS

UK | USA | Canada | Ireland | Australia
India | New Zealand | South Africa

Puffin Books is part of the Penguin Random House group of companies
whose addresses can be found at global.penguinrandomhouse.com.

www.penguin.co.uk
www.puffin.co.uk
www.ladybird.co.uk

First published 2016
'Christmas with the Chrystals' first published 1959 by Basil Blackwell.
Reprinted in *The Puffin Book of Christmas Stories* first published
1984 by Faber and Faber, published in Puffin Books 1986
Author's text including 'My Christmas Holidays' and 'What Happened
to Pauline, Petrova and Posy' published in *The Noel Streatfeild Christmas
Holiday Book* first published 1973 by J. M. Dent
Extract from *Ballet Shoes* first published 1936 by J. M. Dent; extract from
Tennis Shoes first published 1937 by J. M. Dent; extract from *Circus Shoes*,
first published as *The Circus is Coming* 1938 by J. M. Dent; extract from
Theatre Shoes, first published as *Curtain Up* 1944 by J. M. Dent

002

Text copyright © Noel Streatfeild, 1959, 1973
Illustrations in 'Christmas with the Chrystals' by Jill Bennett,
copyright © Jill Bennett, 1959
Illustration from *Ballet Shoes* copyright © Ruth Gervis, 1949
Every effort has been made to trace the owner of the rights for the
artwork by D. L. Mays in *Tennis Shoes* and *Theatre Shoes*. The publisher
would be very glad to hear from the copyright holder.

The moral right of the author and illustrator has been asserted

Typeset in Bembo by Palimpsest Book Production Ltd, Falkirk, Stirlingshire

Printed and bound in Great Britain by Clays Ltd, Elcograf S.p.A.

A CIP catalogue record for this book is available from the British Library

ISBN: 978-0-141-37773-5

All correspondence to:
Puffin Books
Penguin Random House Children's
80 Strand, London WC2R ORL

MIX
Paper from
responsible sources
FSC® C018179
www.fsc.org

Penguin Random House is committed to a
sustainable future for our business, our readers
and our planet. This book is made from Forest
Stewardship Council® certified paper.

Contents

1. Christmas with the Chrystals

'DEAR MUM, I saw the enclosed and thought it might suit you and Dad. Love, Ivy.' The enclosed was an advertisement which read:

Wanted: married couple to take complete charge of kitchen for Christmas. Castle has been rented for large party including several children. Write Box 2060.

Mrs Chrystal read the advertisement at breakfast, and passed it across to her husband, Ted Chrystal.

'I never thought when I wrote to Ivy saying we might take temporary domestic work we'd be away for Christmas.'

Ted always thought well before he spoke.

'Nor me neither,' he agreed at last, 'but I don't see no harm in us writing in. We're used to working of a Christmas, you know, Rosa.'

Rosa took back the advertisement.

'In our own line, yes, but fancy us spending all Christmas in a kitchen – seem funny, wouldn't it?'

There was another pause, during which Ted slowly finished his cup of tea.

'I don't know so much. We've always tried to give kids a good time of a Christmas and this is another way of doing it. You're a beautiful cook, Rosa, and, though I say it as shouldn't, you couldn't want a better kitchen help than your humble.'

Rosa looked rather like an old-fashioned cottage loaf, for she had an almost round body. Now she heaved herself out of her chair, and balanced herself on her short fat legs.

'Whatever you say, Ted, you know that. I'll get the inkpot and write straight away.'

Three days later the Chrystals got a reply to their letter. It was written on very grand stiff cream note-paper, with a London address and telephone number at the top.

Dear Mrs Chrystal,

I am instructed by Mrs Cornelius to reply to your application. You will please both call at the above address on Monday next at 12 noon precisely.

Yours sincerely,
F. SMITH
(*Secretary*)

'I don't know, Ted,' said Rosa, 'that I like the sound of this. There's something about that twelve noon precisely that I don't fancy.'

Ted took the letter, read it, and held it up to the light to see the watermark in the paper. Then he passed it back to Rosa.

'I know what you mean and maybe I don't fancy it myself, but where that paper come from there's money, and we can do with a bit of that, so we'll be there at twelve noon precise come Monday.'

Mrs Cornelius lived in an immensely expensive block of flats not far from Piccadilly. Rosa had on her fur coat, a leftover from better-off days. The fur had an out-all-night look, and the coat no longer met in front, so it had to be worn open, but, as Rosa said to Ted, 'fur gives confidence'.

Under the coat she wore what she called 'me velvet'. This was a plum-coloured dress which had been good once but now, at important places, had a bald look. On her head she wore a small black hat trimmed with a shiny buckle. Ted had on his only suit, steamed and pressed for the occasion, his better shirt carefully pruned by Rosa of threads round the collar and cuffs, and his overcoat. They were not proud of the overcoat, which was definitely past its prime, so it had been their plan to leave it in the hall of the flats while they saw Mrs Cornelius, but the uniformed commissionaire was so terrifically grand and aloof they lost their nerve, and having given the flat number, meekly followed him into the lift, Ted still wearing the coat.

Some women can never make the place where they live look like a home. Others, even if they only spend a night in a room give it a belonging atmosphere. Mrs Cornelius was the first sort of person. Her sitting-room was enormous, with a lovely view from the windows of Green Park. Everything she possessed was rare and expensive; some pieces of her furniture and many of her ornaments should have been in a museum. Every chair and the sofa had cushions without a dent in them, so it was hard to believe anyone sat down. The exquisite desk, though there was a chair in front of it, was obviously never used. In great vases, though it was December, there were formal arrangements of forced spring flowers, which seemed to droop from lack of affection.

Ted and Rosa, having been shown in by a pompous man-servant, waited until the door shut, then they gave each other a look.

'This isn't us, Ted,' Rosa whispered, 'no money wouldn't be worth it.'

Ted answered, for him, quite quickly.

'Shouldn't wonder if you're right, old girl. Pity, we could have done with the money, but it just wouldn't be worth it if we was scared to touch anything.'

A woman came in. She was small, thin, mouse-coloured all over, and nervous as a bird scared, though it is hungry, to pick up a crumb. She spoke in a low, frightened voice.

'Mr and Mrs Chrystal? I'm Miss Smith, Mrs Cornelius's secretary.'

'Pleased, I'm sure,' said Rosa.

Ted gave a faint bow.

'Good morning, Miss.'

'Mrs Cornelius is seeing you herself.' Miss Smith stated this as if she was telling the Chrystals they were to see the Queen.

Her tone gave Rosa courage.

'I don't think we'll be troubling her, thank you.' She was going to explain that she and Ted liked nice things round them, but homely, when she was stopped in the middle of a word by Miss Smith, whose face was wobbling as faces do before the owner cries.

'Oh, please don't say no. I oughtn't to tell you this, but you're the only answer we've had, and we've been advertising for ages, and it's almost Christmas, and how I'm going to manage the castle on my own . . .' The wobble won, tears began rolling down Miss Smith's mouse-coloured face.

'Now, dear,' said Rosa, 'don't take on.'

Ted made shocked clucking noises.

'Maybe we spoke hasty. Mrs Chrystal and me have never been ones to let others down.'

Miss Smith dabbed her eyes.

'So stupid, but you've no idea what is planned, you see . . .' She broke off, turning grey under the mouse colour. 'Here is Mrs Cornelius. Please, please don't tell her I was upset, or what I've said.'

Mrs Cornelius was a woman who might have been seventy, but her face, hair and teeth had for years been so regardlessly looked after and operated on that she could have been younger. She wore a black dress which appeared simple, but an experienced eye would have told it could not have cost less than a hundred pounds. She had wonderful pearls round her neck and a magnificent emerald ring on her finger, and emeralds in her ears. It was not, however, at these things or the frock at which the Chrystals looked, but at Mrs Cornelius's eyes. These were a startlingly vivid blue and hard as a calculating machine. Mrs Cornelius had a voice to match her eyes.

'Are these the couple, Miss Smith?' Miss Smith made a sound which could have been yes. Mrs Cornelius came into the room and sat down. She pointed to the sofa. 'You may sit.'

Gingerly Ted and Rosa sat, terribly conscious as they did so of the dents their behinds were making in the otherwise uncreased sofa. Ted could feel Rosa was nervous and that gave him the courage to be the first to speak.

'My wife is a good cook, but we were just saying to Miss Smith here we were not at all sure we'd be right for this post . . .'

Mrs Cornelius apparently did not hear that.

'I must explain the position for which I may engage you. I have married three times. I gave my first husband a daughter before he died. That daughter is now married, a very poor marriage, I fear. She has two children. My second marriage was to an American. I gave him a son before he died; that son is now dead, but there is a widow with one child. Mr Cornelius came from South Africa; I gave him a son who is married and has three children. It is many years since I saw my own children, I have never seen my son-in-law nor my two daughters-in-law nor my grand-children, so this year I propose to see them all. I have rented Caldecote Castle, which is in Kent, and I am entertaining them for Christmas. You will cook for the household.'

Rosa had been counting on her fingers while Mrs Cornelius was speaking.

'That would mean eleven to cook for, as well as yourself and Miss Smith, making thirteen.'

'That is correct,' Mrs Cornelius agreed, 'but as well there will be Mr Cornelius.'

That surprised both Ted and Rosa, who had taken it for granted Mr Cornelius was as dead as were the other two husbands. Rosa looked round for signs of him, for in her opinion you could always tell when there was a man in the house. She could not see anything male about, but she felt that there was a Mr Cornelius somewhere was good news, for it meant, if they took the job, there would be someone else to work for besides Mrs Cornelius.

'That makes a difference, doesn't it, Ted?'

Mrs Cornelius turned the full blaze of her eyes on Rosa.

'I cannot imagine why Mr Cornelius should make a difference, for it is many years since we met.'

There was a pause, while Rosa and Ted digested that. Then Ted said, 'Fourteen plus staff I suppose.'

'Dailies only, so no meals,' Mrs Cornelius stated firmly.

Ted shook his head, for he was by now determined not to allow his Rosa to endure Mrs Cornelius.

'All the same, it'll be too much for the wife.' He got up. 'I'm sorry we've taken up your time. Come along, Rosa.'

Miss Smith gave a sound between a sob and a moan. Rosa, as she heaved herself up from the soft depths of the sofa, looked at her with compassion.

'Don't take on, dear, but fourteen is a lot and we're not as young as we were.'

Mrs Cornelius gave Miss Smith a look which, had she seen it, would have shrivelled her.

'Be quiet you foolish creature.' She held up a hand. 'One moment, you two. I realize the work will be hard, so if you are willing to go to the castle on Friday next to prepare and lay in stores, and to remain until the 28th, I will pay you over and above all expenses one hundred pounds.'*

One hundred pounds! To Rosa and Ted that was a fortune, magic money which others had but never you. Why, however hard the work, with a hundred pounds they could afford to get over it with a little holiday. Ted nudged Rosa to show she should answer.

'Very well, Mrs Cornelius, if you would put the offer in writing, we'll come.'

Miss Smith and the Chrystals arrived together on the following Friday. The castle, they discovered, though it was partly lived in sometimes by the

---

* In 1958, when this story was written, £100 was worth a great deal more than it is today.

owners, was mostly a museum, and it is difficult to make museums homely for a Christmas party. Mrs Cornelius was using only one wing, but that had thirty bedrooms, a vast drawing-room, a dining-room, which looked as though it should have belonged to a city company, a billiard room, and many smaller rooms. It had, too, a great central staircase and long passages most inadequately heated.

'The temperature in Mrs Cornelius's part of the castle is never to drop below seventy degrees,' said Miss Smith through chattering teeth.

Rosa had her own troubles with a great draughty kitchen, but she still had kindness to spare for Miss Smith.

'You can only do your best, dear. I reckon if you get the chill off the place it'll be a miracle.'

But it is wonderful what can be done when there is unlimited money to spend, and by midday on Saturday there were fires in every fireplace, and oil stoves in chilly corners, and an old man who lived nearby was bribed at an enormous wage to do nothing but keep the stoves and fires going.

Miss Smith contrived other miracles. Nobody wants to work over Christmas, especially not housewives with their own families to think of, but Christmas is an expensive time, and so Miss

Smith, with persuasion and offering unheard-of pay, organized a small regiment of women willing to work in shifts starting on the Monday morning.

Rosa and Ted would not have any help as they felt there would have to be a good deal of muddling through, and if that was to happen they would rather it was when there was no one watching. One of their troubles was the food. Rosa prided herself on her cooking, but some of the things sent for the store cupboard she had never heard of or seen before. There were tins of strange tropical fruits. There were great chunks of dried turtle – looking for all the world like blocks of amber. Did people really drink soup made of kangaroos' tails? They had, of course, heard of *pâté de foie gras*, but how did you serve it? The same applied to caviare; never had Rosa supposed caviare was sold in such enormous tins. Then there were cases of Christmas delicacies. Was the cook expected to arrange all the exotic little eats, and, if so, on what?

'Thank God I brought my *Mrs Beeton*,' Rosa confided to Ted; 'if I'm properly stuck she'll see me through.'

Mrs Cornelius arrived in the morning. Until she came into the castle there had been a happy bustle as Miss Smith's first shift of women came in and began cleaning and polishing. The women knew each other, and there were jokes and whistling and snatches of singing. But the moment Mrs Cornelius came in it was as if the icy wind from outside came with her. She made a tour of inspection, and though she said very little, and even gave a word of praise – 'Your arrangements appear satisfactory, Miss Smith' – as she went round the castle, the Christmas feeling seemed to slip out through the doors and windows.

Rosa and Ted had by now made the kitchen their home. It was gay with Christmas cards, for another large batch had arrived that morning, and Ted had found some holly in the grounds and had stuck branches over the clock and on the dresser. Then there was Rosa's old thumbed *Mrs Beeton* on the table, and Rosa's large overalls hanging on the kitchen door. So it was not into an unlived characterless room that Mrs Cornelius stepped when she visited the kitchen, but into a warm, rich-smelling place, full of atmosphere.

Rosa and Ted had been practising for that moment, and though they had laughed a lot they had it planned to perfection.

'Good morning, Madam, welcome to Caldecote Castle,' said Ted with a deep bow.

Rosa, for all her cottage-loaf shape, managed a bob of a curtsy.

'And the compliments of the season, Madam; I hope you have a wonderful Christmas.'

This welcome sounded so like a scene from an old-fashioned play that Mrs Cornelius gave each of the Chrystals a look from her hard blue eyes to see if the welcome was intended as insolence. But it clearly was not, for both Rosa and Ted returned her look with expressions of such goodwill it was obvious, odd though it might seem, that they meant what they had said.

Mrs Cornelius did not reply to the goodwill wishes, but they did something to her, for she did not say the words that had been on her lips when she came in: 'Take down those cards and that holly. This is a kitchen, not an amusement arcade.' Instead she went straight to giving her orders.

'I shall have a light lunch. All my guests will be here for tea. Miss Smith has, I believe, given you the menu for dinner tonight?'

'Yes, Madam,' said Rosa.

'Then that I think is all.' Mrs Cornelius turned to go, but Rosa stopped her.

'What about the children?'

'What about them?'

'Well, children won't be eating oysters and that at eight o'clock like you've ordered,' Rosa explained. 'Are they to have supper, or something for their tea?'

It was so long since Mrs Cornelius had met a child, and even her own she had never seen eat that she could remember, so she did not know what Rosa meant.

'Something for their tea? What can you have for tea other than cake, scones and sandwiches?'

Ted saw he must help Rosa.

'Miss Smith told us the eldest child is fourteen and the youngest seven; that means special food, Madam, and a sit-down tea.'

'A glass of milk and biscuits or that for the little ones in bed,' Rosa added, 'but something light but tasty for the others, they won't want to upset their stomachs with what's going into the dining-room.'

Mrs Cornelius looked and felt as if she was having something unpleasant told to her.

'I am really not interested in what or when the children eat. I will instruct Miss Smith to find out from the parents what is required and she will inform you.'

Once more Rosa and Ted managed the bow and bob they had rehearsed. Then, as the door closed behind Mrs Cornelius, Rosa covered her mouth with her hand to hold back the big laugh that rose like a fountain in her.

'She'll be the death of me, Ted.'

Ted's eyes were twinkling.

'Come on, my old trouble, for she'll be the death of both of us if her light lunch isn't served pronto.'

Virginia, the daughter Mrs Cornelius told the Chrystals she had given her first husband, had, by her mother's standards, made a poor marriage. For she had married Tom Oswald, who not only had no money of his own, but was not much good at earning it. Mrs Cornelius, when Virginia had collected sufficient courage to tell her whom she was marrying, had been so disgusted she had refused to attend the wedding, and had not seen Virginia since. But though her mother might think Tom Oswald a poor sort of husband, Virginia knew him to be a perfect one, for he was warm, loving, and of a happy disposition, all qualities she had been unused to in her own home. Tom was a gardener, a job that was not well paid but at which he was very good. Where Tom gardened there was a cottage, and in it Virginia's and Tom's children, Alan and Benita, had grown up to the ages of fourteen and twelve without ever seeing or thinking about their Cornelius grandmother.

It had been one of the few mornings that the Oswalds' cottage had not been full of laughter when the invitation arrived to spend Christmas in Caldecote Castle. Tom and Virginia, for the sake of the children, tried not to show how depressed and frightened the letter of invitation made them, but they were not successful, for Alan and Benita were intelligent.

'Must we go?' Alan asked. 'She's never bothered with us before.'

'Christmas is always perfect here,' Benita pleaded. 'Don't let's go.'

Mrs Cornelius would not have believed her ears if she could have heard Tom's answer to his children.

'Poor old lady. We mustn't be selfish, we have so much and she's got nothing. Let's give her one nice Christmas to remember.'

Mrs Cornelius's second husband had been a Mr Silas P. Dawson, an American. By him she had a son called James. Mr Dawson had been immensely rich and it had been his intention that James should be rich too, but he had died while James was a small child and so had left his fortune to his wife, expecting her to provide for James. And so she would have done if James had behaved as she expected him to. But James had not, for he had fallen in love with a pretty penniless school teacher, and insisted on marrying her, and a year later had died, leaving behind him a baby son called Gardiner. Mrs Cornelius felt that James's death relieved her of responsibility. 'That girl Lalla he married,' she told herself, 'supported herself as a teacher before she married him, so I suppose she can continue to do so. I will, however, provide for Gardiner in my will.'

That keeping yourself as a school teacher was one thing, and keeping yourself and a baby son was another had not struck Mrs Cornelius, and Lalla, who was proud, would not write to explain and ask for help. Instead, somehow she managed, and though she and Gardiner lived in two rooms in downtown New York, which were far too hot in summer and dismally cold in winter, they not only managed to survive but to enjoy themselves.

Gardiner had scarcely heard of Grandmother Cornelius, but he was wild with excitement at the thought of the journey by jet plane, which was part of the invitation.

'Gee, a jet plane! Will that be something to tell the other boys!'

Mrs Cornelius's living husband, old Hans Cornelius, lived outside Cape Town in an exquisite white Cape Dutch house. Just a couple of miles away his son Jan lived in another beautiful house with his wife Anna and their three children, Peter who was ten, and the two little girls, Jane who was eight and Rinke seven.

Christmas comes in the summer in South Africa, so when Jan drove over with Anna to show his father their letter from Mrs Cornelius, they found him in his rose garden, which was in full flower.

Old Hans smelt a glorious golden rose before he gave his opinion.

'I would like to say no. Why should we leave our beautiful South Africa to go to cold foggy England? But your mother, Jan, is no longer young and no doubt lonely, so if you can make the sacrifice, Anna, my dear, I think we should all go, for it will be a treat for her to see your children.'

The families arrived at the castle within half an hour of each other. The first to get there were

Gardiner and his mother. Miss Smith, trying by the warmth of her smile to build her small mouse-coloured self into a whole reception committee, met them in the hall and showed them to their rooms, and, as she did so, her spirits bounded upwards. For in Lalla she saw not a frightening, demanding American daughter-in-law belonging to Mrs Cornelius, but a tired young woman, with a face prematurely lined from standing too long hours in the store where she worked, and with hair turning grey from the worry of making ends meet. And so Miss Smith did something she had never dreamed she would be doing to one of the daughters-in-law, she put an arm through Lalla's and said: 'You must rest while you are here. I shall see you have breakfast in bed every day.'

Alan and Benita, as soon as they arrived, were turned out of their rooms by their mother who, looking at the vast amount of cupboard space, had decided she would unpack for the family, and so, by skilful laying out and hanging up, disguise how few clothes they possessed. So Gardiner, prowling along a passage, ran slap into them.

''Lo,' he said, pleasantly surprised by Alan's appearance, for he had on his grey flannel trousers and he had supposed all English boys wore short pants. 'I'm Gardiner. You'll be Alan and Benita. Gee, this is a big place and unfriendly some way.'

'Have the others come, the South African ones?' Benita asked.

Gardiner dismissed the Cornelius children.

'Naw. Come on, let's explore.'

It was exploring that took Alan, Benita and Gardiner into the kitchen. They reached it by way of the thickly carpeted front hall, where every corner was set with formally staged groups of pot plants.

'Like a funeral parlour,' Gardiner whispered. 'How say we see what's through this green door?'

To the children the kitchen was immediately home. Rosa and Ted were having an early cup of tea, and without invitation the three pulled up chairs and joined them.

'How come,' Gardiner asked, looking appreciatively at the cards and holly, 'you've got all this out here and we've got nothing back there?'

Rosa passed him a cup of tea.

'You're seeing your Granny after tea. I'm sure you've only got to ask and she'll send for a tree and holly and that.'

Benita, relaxing for the first time since she had reached the castle, took the slice of cake Ted offered her.

'It's not that we need a tree exactly, but it's not like Christmas without one. At home Dad cuts down a tree and we all decorate it.'

'I daresay your Dad could do the same here,' said Ted, 'there's plenty of trees in the grounds.'

Alan shook his head.

'I don't reckon Dad would face up to that. Out there,' he pointed vaguely towards the front of the castle, 'it's like a posh hotel, you couldn't mess it up, and you can't trim a tree without mess.'

The Cornelius children might be small but they were bright. So while their mother was unpacking, cheeping like sparrows and as if they had always known the castle, they hurried along the bedroom corridor, down the main staircase, through the baize covered door which divided the kitchen world from the rest of the house, straight to Rosa, Ted and their new cousins. They stood in the doorway, beaming.

'Hullo,' said Peter, 'I'm Peter, this is Jane and this is Rinke. We're hungry.'

Rosa fetched some more cups from where they were hanging on the dresser.

'Bring up three chairs, Ted. Do you drink milk or tea, dears?'

When the children were fetched by Miss Smith to come to the drawing-room, something made the six know they must not tell Grandmother Cornelius that they had made friends with the Chrystals. Instead they told her about each other, to the great amusement of old Hans Cornelius, who was watching Mrs Cornelius's face.

After they had all been introduced Rinke said, 'Do you know, Grandmother Cornelius, Benita's father is a gardener, which means they can have all the vegetables they need, which is lucky, for they can't often have meat.'

'Imagine that,' Jane added. 'We have meat every day, don't you, Grandmother Cornelius?'

'Gardiner's mother works in a store,' Peter piped up, 'so Gardiner's always had to get his own lunch. He makes sandwiches of anything that's in the ice box; when there isn't much he makes do with bread.'

Gardiner thought that was enough about him. He jerked his head towards the three Cornelius children and gave a wink.

'They were wondering how Santa gets to find his way in a place this size, but I told them he'd figure it out, that's right, isn't it?'

'We were wondering about a tree, Grandmother Cornelius,' Benita said softly. 'I mean, it needn't cost anything, I'm sure there's one about Dad could cut down.'

'And we could make the ornaments,' Alan suggested hopefully, 'fir cones and that, painted.'

Mrs Cornelius, who had been silenced by the shower of talk, made a signal to Miss Smith.

'Order a tree and tell them to send decorations, and people to hang them up.'

'And there ought to be masses and masses of parcels in coloured paper,' Jane prompted, 'there always are.'

Mrs Cornelius had not had a Christmas present for so long she had forgotten about them. She gave another signal to Miss Smith.

'And order parcels suitably packed.'

Twelve eyes stared at her. Rinke spoke for them all.

'That,' she said firmly, 'is not the way to buy Christmas presents. You choose them.'

Gardiner looked round the beautifully furnished but unlived-in room.

'Don't you get cards at Christmas, Grandmother Cornelius?'

Miss Smith caught old Hans Cornelius's eye. It said: 'That's enough for one night. Take them away.' Miss Smith took the hint.

'Come along, dears. It's time you younger ones went to bed,' and she swept the children out of the room.

The grown-ups' dinner having been served and washed up, the Chrystals, Alan, Benita and Gardiner sat down to their own supper. A splendid meal where everybody ate something different, and all helped themselves. And it was then that the children learned something strange. It came out when Rosa and Ted were showing them their Christmas cards.

'Why,' Benita asked, 'does this one say "To the best goose that ever laid a golden egg"?'

Ted looked at Rosa, who smiled cosily back at him.

'Tell them. They won't say anything and they'll like to hear.'

'Well, it's this way,' said Ted. 'I've been an actor all my life.'

'And none better,' put in Rosa.

'But my speciality was animals.'

'More especially geese,' said Rosa. 'I reckon there's never been a goose in panto to touch him.'

Rosa and Ted, helped out by Alan and Benita, had to explain to Gardiner what a pantomime was, and then he found it hard to believe there were such entertainments.

'The mother's a man called a dame, the principal man is played by a girl, and you come on as a goose. I haven't seen nothing yet!'

It was with difficulty Rosa and Ted urged the children to bed, for they knew they must be tired, and they themselves had a long, hard day ahead of them.

'I tell you what, though,' said Rosa, 'tomorrow I'll get Miss Smith to buy paper for making paper-rings; we always had them when I was a child.'

'That's right,' Ted agreed, 'smashing decorations they make.'

'Even the little ones can make them,' Rosa went on, 'and while you're doing it Ted shall tell you about working in a pantomime.'

To the dismay of the adults the next day was hopelessly wet, so wet that even the men could only manage a short walk in the dripping castle grounds. But the children did not mind how much it rained. All the morning they were busy, helping to prepare the lunch; then when they had eaten a splendid meal themselves, the paper for ring-making arrived and they settled round a table with a vast pot of paste made by Rosa, and Ted sat with them, talking in his slow way about pantomimes. Sometimes he demonstrated.

'Then I'd come to the footlights, like this; wonderful music I had for that bit, and acted like I was heartbroken, see, for I was turned out, me that was part of the family.'

Rosa hummed Ted's goose music, and Ted, in spite of the fact that he was wearing ordinary trousers held up over his shirt by braces, and an apron tied round him, seemed to the children to become a goose.

During tea, Ted, helped out by Rosa, imitated principal boys they had known, and to see him swaggering up and down the kitchen as if he was a lovely girl with magnificent legs in tights was really something. So it was to a kitchen echoing with laughter that Miss Smith came from the sad bridge-playing drawing-room to fetch the children to see their grandmother. It was after this visit that they decided to keep their decorations a secret.

'Good evening, children,' said Mrs Cornelius. 'What have you been doing today?'

The children had not planned what to answer if they were asked that, so Peter said, 'Playing.'

'When is the tree being erected?' Mrs Cornelius asked Miss Smith.

'Now,' Miss Smith twittered. 'It can be lighted tonight.'

'Trees,' said Jane, 'aren't lighted until Christmas Eve. That's when you have your presents.'

Alan disagreed with that.

'We don't have ours till Christmas Day.'

'We don't get a tree,' Gardiner broke in. 'Mum can't afford one.'

In the little silence that fell after that old Hans Cornelius looked at Mrs Cornelius.

'We wouldn't have one either if Dad didn't get it free,' said Benita.

On the way back to the kitchen the children had a small committee meeting.

'Let's keep our rings for the kitchen part of the castle,' Peter suggested. 'It's much the nicest bit.'

Alan had another idea. 'And I'll find a little tree in the grounds, there's heaps of room for it at the end of the kitchen.'

The Chrystals were delighted when they heard what was planned.

'Oh, I would like a tree,' said Rosa, 'it's years since I had one. And I tell you what we'll do, we'll put the lights out on Christmas Eve and light the tree and leave the curtains undrawn; they say you should always have lights in the window on a Christmas Eve to show the Christ Child the way.'

Rinke put her arms as far as they would go round Rosa.

'Darling, darling Rosa, could we sing carols round your tree?'

'It's the only place we could,' Alan pointed out, 'carols would sound all wrong in any other part of the castle.'

The tree, decorated quietly and efficiently by girls and men sent with it, was lit that evening. When it was finished, Miss Smith, who had long ago become 'Smithy' to the children, dug them out of the kitchen to admire it.

'Mrs Cornelius will want to know that you've seen it.'

'It's a very neat tree,' said Jane.

Benita looked up at the shining new decorations.

'It seems as if it felt embarrassed here.'

Alan was looking at the parcels under the tree.

'Smithy, how will Grandmother Cornelius know which is for which?' he asked. 'There's no labels.'

'They've left a chart, dear,' Miss Smith explained. 'Blue paper for men. Green for women. Red for boys. Yellow for girls.'

Jane started to move back towards the kitchen. 'Just like a Santa does in a shop.'

It was that night that the first grown-up dared to break out from the drawing-room. It was old Hans Cornelius; he was not playing in the rubber of bridge which was going on, so he slipped quietly out of the room, and, like a homing pigeon, found his way through the green baize door. The Chrystals, Alan, Benita and Gardiner were having Welsh rarebit for supper, and while they ate it Ted was describing a night when the curtain had stuck and would not come down at the end of *Dick Whittington*.

'And there was Miss Dolores Dear, always one to be upset easily, stepping forward and saying:

"And now we've had enough of this and that,

"Let's say farewell to Whittington . . ."
and that was where I had to come forward for the "and cat", but the curtain stuck, so she starts again and . . .'

Old Hans had come in so quietly that at first they did not see him standing in the doorway. Then he said, 'That Welsh rarebit smells very good, Mrs Chrystal. Could I have a bit?'

Old Hans told Jan where he had been, and Jan told Anna, and Anna told Lalla, and Lalla told Virginia, who, of course, passed on the news to Tom. So the next day, which was Christmas Eve, there was great rivalry amongst the grown-ups to cut out of the bridge rubbers, for it was so lovely and Christmassy in the kitchen, with paper-rings festooned across the ceiling and a jolly little tree in the window.

'And tonight we're going to light it,' said Rinke.

'And leave the curtains open,' Jane explained.

'Rosa says it's to show Jesus the way to come,' Gardiner added.

'If you can get out of playing bridge, Mummy,' Benita implored, 'do come here after dinner, for that's when we shall sing carols.'

'The kids,' Alan explained, nodding at Peter, Jane and Rinke, 'are coming down in their dressing-gowns.'

'I'll be there somehow,' Virginia promised.

'I wouldn't miss it,' said old Hans.

'Nor us,' Jan and Anna agreed.

'Count on me,' Tom stated firmly.

'What about you?' Gardiner asked his mother.

'I'll be there,' said Lalla.

So that evening, after dinner, on one excuse and another, everybody slipped out of the drawing-room and away to the kitchen, until Mrs Cornelius, with the cards in front of her, had no one with whom to play bridge. She rang the bell for Miss Smith, but Miss Smith, enraptured, was in the kitchen and did not hear it. Furiously Mrs Cornelius rang again, and again nobody came. So, determined to tell everybody what she thought of them, she left the drawing-room and marched out into the great hall. She might, and very nearly did, miss opening the green baize door, but something guided her to it.

Standing unseen, looking into the kitchen, Mrs Cornelius forgot the angry things she had meant to say. In the window was the little tree, nothing like so grand as the one in the hall, but bright with lights. All round it stood her family, with Miss Smith and the Chrystals. They were singing 'Good King Wenceslas', old Hans' voice booming as the king.

Bring me flesh and bring me wine,
Bring me pine-logs hither;
Thou and I will see him dine,
When we bear them thither.

Everybody sang the next lines, and then Gardiner's shrill treble rang out:

Sire, the night is darker now,
And the wind blows stronger,
Fails my heart, I know not how
I can go no longer.

It was as if Mrs Cornelius's heart had been made of ice, and now suddenly the ice was melting. She was not cross, she was envious. She wanted more than she had wanted anything for years to feel she could join that party round the tree, and not by her mere presence spoil the beauty of the evening for everybody else. She meant to go back to the drawing-room, and would have gone, but as she moved, a board creaked and, just as Mrs Cornelius had feared, the carol-singing faltered. But Rosa and Ted were not having that.

'Madam!' Rosa said, making room for her.

'Come on, Madam,' Ted added.

Mrs Cornelius came on and found herself singing words she had forgotten she had ever known.

> *Therefore, Christian men, be sure,*
> *Wealth or rank possessing,*
> *Ye who now will bless the poor,*
> *Shall yourselves find blessing.*

Ballet Shoes

When Noel Streatfeild wrote *Ballet Shoes* she
had no idea how popular it was to become.
Here she introduces the story to children who
may not have read it, and this is followed by an
extract in which the three Fossil sisters are
encouraged to save up for their futures.

2. An Introduction to *Ballet Shoes*

*P*EOPLE LIKE *me who write books often get letters from strangers. The letters are of all types, but by far the largest are written by people who want to know what happens next to some characters in a book in whom they have become interested. The real answer is nothing happens next. An author has planned what his or her book is about and when they reach the end that, as far as they are concerned, is the finish. Of course this does not apply to authors who write serials: they can write perhaps as many as six books about the same characters.*

Of all the books I have written none has brought in as many requests for a sequel as a book I wrote called Ballet Shoes. *For those of you* who have not read it, the story is about three babies who were adopted by an old man who collected fossils. His name was Great Uncle Matthew or G.U.M. for short.

Great Uncle Matthew had a great-niece who lived with him in a house in the Cromwell Road, London. She was called Sylvia, and she and her old nurse, called Nana, together with a cook and a housemaid called Clara, ran the house for Gum. This, in his fossil-collecting days, was quite a job, for he travelled a lot and brought back hundreds of fossils, some very large which he parked all over the house. In fact the house would have been full of fossils and nothing else if it had not been for Nana, who now and then would make Sylvia tell her uncle that not another fossil came into the house until a large number had gone out. Gum hated parting with a fossil, but when Nana got firm he had to. Then workmen would arrive with crates and in time there would be a notice in The Times saying that Professor Matthew Brown had given another generous gift of fossils to a museum.

One year poor Gum, when fossil-hunting on a mountain, had a terrible fall, as a result of which he lost a leg. That put an end to his fossil-hunting for good but not to his travels, for he decided to

*see the world by sea. That is how the first baby
came to the house. Gum's ship struck an iceberg
and all the passengers had to take to the boats.
One of the boats overturned and everybody
was drowned except a baby found cooing in a
life belt. Gum, used to collecting things, picked up
the baby, wrapped her in his coat and, when they
were rescued, took her to the Cromwell Road.*

*The baby was christened Pauline after St Paul
who, you remember, had also been rescued from
the sea. Gum argued a bit because he wanted her
called after a famous fossil, but Nana said:*

*'Babies in my nurseries, sir, never have had
outlandish names, and they're not starting now.
Miss Sylvia has chosen a nice sensible name, and
called after a blessed saint, and no other name is
going to be used, if you'll forgive me speaking
plain, sir.'*

*A year later Gum turned up with a second
baby. He had found this one in a hospital where
he had gone to have urgent treatment for his leg.
There he made friends with a poor young Russian
whose wife had died giving birth when her baby
was born. To Gum it was a matter of course,
when the young Russian also died, that he should
adopt the baby.*

'We have a baby at home that I have adopted,' he said. 'We shall have another.'

The new baby was called Petrova. Nana accepted her quite calmly.

'Very nice for Pauline to have a companion,' then she added: 'Let's hope this one has brains, for it's easy to see who's going to be Miss Plain in my nursery.'

But to Gum she spoke very firmly.

'Now, sir – two babies in the nursery is right and proper, and such as the best homes have a right to expect, but two is enough. Bring one more and I give notice.'

Probably it was fear of what Nana would say that made Gum send the third and last baby by district messenger. She arrived in a basket and with her came a note and a little pair of ballet shoes. Gum said in the note that he was sorry not to bring the baby himself, but he was off on a friend's yacht to visit some strange island. He was expecting to be away for some years. He had arranged for the bank to see Sylvia had all the money she needed for five years. About the baby he said that her mother was a dancer and her name was Posy, to which he added: 'Unfortunate but true.'

About four months later a parcel arrived addressed to 'The Little Fossils'. In it were three necklaces – a turquoise one for Pauline, a string of tiny seed pearls for Petrova and a string of coral for Posy.

'Well,' said Nana, 'I expect that's the last of him we shall hear for some time.'

She was quite right.

Gum did not come back in five years, so the bank stopped paying Sylvia money. To help out she took in boarders: two Doctors of Literature, a Mr and Mrs Simpson from Malaya and a Miss Theo Dane who taught dancing at The Children's Academy of Dancing and Stage Training.

It was these boarders who changed the children's lives. Theo Dane got them into the theatrical school where she taught. Mr Simpson encouraged Petrova in her love of engines and the Doctors of Literature gave the children lessons. Still Gum didn't come home and often money was very tight, so as soon as Pauline and Petrova were old enough they became professional child actors. Posy, who was the dancer of the family, did not appear professionally, for she was not old enough when the book finished.

3. Independence at Fourteen

'A MIDSUMMER Night's Dream' was a success. It had been hoped in producing it late in September that it would run until the theatre put on a Christmas production. It did better than that: it ran over Christmas with matinées every day. Pauline and Petrova got two pounds a week each as fairies; for the extra matinées they got an eighth of their two pounds, so that they got five shillings extra for each matinée, which brought their salaries up to three pounds a week. They had been putting one pound into the post office, sending four shillings to the Academy, giving ten shillings to Sylvia for the house, which left six shillings a week for clothes and pocket money, which was not much, with all the clothes they needed, and they very seldom got any pocket money, and never more than a penny or twopence. Their extra matinée money came as a surprise; it was in their pay envelopes, and they were not expecting it. A whole pound more; it seemed immense wealth. Naturally two shillings of it went to the Academy; but that would still leave eighteen.

'Do you think, Nana,' Pauline asked, 'that if we gave Garnie another ten shillings, and you had five for our clothes we could have the extra for spending; that's six shillings between us, which would be two shillings a week each?'

Nana shook her head.

'I doubt it, dear, with all that's needed for you. What do you want two shillings for?'

Pauline fingered her pay envelope. She hesitated to tell Nana her secret ambition, in case she was told it could not be.

'It's theatres,' she explained at last. 'I never go to any. I want to see the good people act. I'd like to go to a matinée every week, when I'm not working. I could if I saved up all my two shillings.'

'Theatres!' Petrova looked disgusted. 'What a waste of good money! If I had two shillings a week, I'd buy books and books and books.'

'And what books!' Pauline remarked bitterly, as both she and Posy disliked Petrova's idea of a library. 'All dull things about engines.'

'Well, there's no need to quarrel about what you'd do with two shillings,' Nana put in, 'for you won't get it; and if you don't hurry, you won't be out of the theatre on time, and that'll get me into trouble with the stage manager, and him with the London County Council, and you'll find yourselves without a job, and then nobody will get two shillings.'

The discussion of the extra pound was brought up at breakfast the next morning. Sylvia, in a way, took Pauline's side; but she insisted that the ten shillings they had planned for the house must go into the post office.

Pauline gave an angry jab at her porridge.

'But that's mean, you know you've got to have the ten shillings, or we couldn't take the two shillings; it's only pretending we could have it if you say that, because you know we wouldn't take it.'

Sylvia took a piece of toast.

'There is just one rule that I won't break, and that is that half what you earn goes into the post office.'

'It didn't when I earned two pounds ten shillings,' Pauline argued. 'Only one pound went into the post office, and you had fifteen shillings, and ten shillings bought clothes.'

'That's true,' Sylvia agreed. 'I told Nana that she could have ten shillings for your clothes that once, but I didn't like it; I was quite ashamed of your savings book, when we took it down to the County Hall.'

Pauline was red with temper.

'Oh, well, if you're going to care what they think.'

'I do,' Sylvia said quietly. 'But I care still more that you have a nice lot saved for when you are grown-up. Now don't let's argue any more about that pound, or we shall all be sorry you are earning it. Ten shillings of it will go into your savings, two shillings to the Academy, five towards your clothes, and two shillings pocket money for each of you.'

'Couldn't you have the five shillings instead of our clothes, Garnie?' Petrova suggested.

Sylvia sighed.

'That would be nice; but you want clothes so badly. Nana says that you all need shoes, and Pauline's got to have a coat. Up till Christmas all she's had is two pounds fourteen from each of you, and when you grow so fast, that goes a very little way. She told me yesterday "A Midsummer Night's Dream" would have to run for months to buy all you need.'

Pauline pushed back her porridge bowl.

'I'm not putting any more in the post office.'

Sylvia, Petrova, and Posy stared at her.

'A child,' Posy recited, 'has-to-put-at-least-one-third-of-its-earnings-in-the-savings-bank, or-as-much-more-as-may-be-directed-by-its-parents-or-guardian. This-is-the-law. I learnt that in French with Madame Moulin, I forget what the French was, but that was what it meant in English.'

Pauline looked braver than she felt.

'It's quite right. That is the law; but I'm not a child. I've just had my fourteenth birthday. The law lets me work; I don't need a licence, and I can do what I like with my own money.'

'Pauline!' Petrova was shocked. 'You wouldn't be so mean as to take it all.'

'You are a fool.' Pauline looked scornful. 'You know I wouldn't. But I was thinking in bed last night; here we are, never any money, Garnie always worried, and we never have any clothes. If the money that I always have to put in the post office is spent on the house and us, we'll have enough. All I want is the two shillings a week for ourselves. I know it sounds a lot, but theatres are expensive – even the gallery.'

Petrova looked at Sylvia.

'It is a good idea, Garnie. She needn't put any more in the post office, need she?'

'I think it's a very good plan,' Posy agreed. 'If I have two shillings I shall save it till next summer and go and see the ballet at Covent Garden. I could go often for that.'

Sylvia looked at them all in a worried way.

'Do get it into your heads that nobody wants to stop you having two shillings to spend. I have always thought it a shame that Pauline had so little for herself when she worked so hard, and now the same applies to you, Petrova. But it must not come out of the half you save. You give me plenty for the house, I can manage.'

'I shall put nothing more into the post office – at least, not until Gum comes home,' Pauline said firmly. 'And what's more, if we need it, I'll take out what I've saved.'

Petrova and Posy looked at her with a mixture of admiration and shocked amazement. If there was anything that was sacred in the family, it was the savings books. The walk to the post office on Saturday mornings was more sure to happen than church on Sunday. Sometimes Nana, after an anxious evening patching and darning, would sigh as she saw the notes swallowed over the post-office counter; but when Petrova one day described the post office as 'that nasty office eating my money' she had been furious.

'Right's right, dear, and it's no good questioning it, and don't let me hear you at it again.'

Now here was Pauline saying she would put nothing more into her book. That she was fourteen and could do as she liked.

Sylvia got up.

'I shall talk to Nana; she's certain to make you see sense, Pauline. The London County Council don't mean that because they give up watching you that they expect me to as well. I've got to take more trouble, if possible.'

Sylvia sent for Nana to come down and talk to her, and as well the two doctors, as they had educated Pauline, and Theo because she taught her dancing. She would have liked to have asked Mrs Simpson's advice too, but she could not think of any excuse. As soon as they all arrived she told them about the money argument and asked what they thought. To her great surprise they agreed with Pauline; but all for different reasons. Theo, who was just dashing off to the Academy, gave her views first. She said that she thought it was important that Petrova should save all she could, as she saw no future for her in the theatre; but that in Pauline's case she showed signs that her gifts as an actress were not those of a precocious child, her work was improving, as incidentally were her looks; she thought with any luck she should be so successful as not to need her savings.

Doctor Jakes and Doctor Smith did not believe in too much saving. They both believed that with more money in the house there would be a chance for the girls to develop their tastes; it would certainly be good for Pauline to be able to go to the theatre now and then. Nana said that she had been feeling in her bones lately there was a change coming. Pauline was getting very independent, and that if it took the form of wanting to help more, she thought she should be given a chance.

Sylvia thanked them, and when they had gone she called Pauline, and told her that she was to have her way.

'Though you know, darling, I'm going to feel dreadful living on you like that.'

Pauline took far more pleasure in her salary now that most of it did not vanish into the post office. It was with dismay that two or three weeks later she heard that the notice was to go up the following Friday. Sure enough when they arrived for the performance on the next Friday there was the notice on the green baize board in the passage. Petrova made a face at it, for although the extra matinées had stopped after three weeks, and they now only had them on Tuesdays and Thursdays, Pauline was still giving them a shilling, but if the play came off shillings were bound to end. Pauline did not seem much depressed about the notice when it was actually up, but rather excited instead. When they went down for their first entrance, Petrova wanted to know if anything nice had happened. She whispered because they were on the side of the stage.

'Not yet,' Pauline whispered back. 'I'll tell you on the way home.'

The matron frowned at them.

'Don't talk in the wings, Pauline and Petrova.'

In the tube that night Pauline dragged at Petrova by the hand and pulled her into one of the seats for two. The one opposite was full, so Nana had to sit some way off, and could not hear what they said. Pauline spoke quickly as she was excited.

'That man that plays Oberon.'

Petrova nodded.

'Donald Houghton?'

'Yes, him. Well, he's putting on "Richard the Third" as soon as this comes off.' She looked at Petrova as if expecting signs of intelligence, but

Petrova gave none. 'Don't you know your "Richard the Third"?'

Pauline sighed at Petrova's short memory.

'You know I don't; you only did it because it was in the test examination you did for your school certificate. What about him doing it?'

'The Princes in the Tower are in it.'

'Us?'

Pauline nodded.

'I don't see why not. I thought we'd ask him.'

'How could we?' Petrova protested. 'We only see him on the stage, and we aren't allowed to go into the grown-ups' dressing-rooms.'

'I thought we'd write.'

Petrova looked in admiration at Pauline.

'That's an idea. When shall we write it?'

Pauline considered their crowded days.

'Well, we might get Theo to let us off dancing practice if we said it was for something very important; but then Posy would want to know what we were doing; and we mustn't tell anybody or we shan't be allowed to send the letter. We shan't have time at lessons, of course, and then there's our walk, then it's half past one. Sometimes there's a quarter of an hour after lunch before our other walk; if there is, we could do it then. If there isn't we'll have to ask the doctors to give us ten minutes out of after-walk lessons, for there's never a minute between them and tea-supper before we go to the theatre.'

'How about us both writing one in our baths and comparing them? That would save time,' Petrova suggested.

The letter which they finally took to the theatre next day was the result of snatched minutes. Theo would not let them off practice, but she gave them five minutes at the end before they began lessons. They got another five minutes after lunch before their walk. Pauline copied the letter out beautifully at evening lessons when she was supposed to be writing an essay. She showed it to Petrova on the tube, and they agreed it could not well be improved upon.

> '*DEAR MR HOUGHTON,*
>
> '*We hear you are going to act King Richard the Third. Would you have us as the Princes? You will not know our names, but we are Pease-blossom and Mustard-seed. We are not supposed to write letters to people in the theatre so would you be sure to send the answer before the last act as we go then. Nana who comes to the*

*theatre with us won't mind but the real Matrons
would.*

'*Yours sincerely,*
'*PAULINE FOSSIL.*'
'*PETROVA FOSSIL.*'

The letter was addressed clearly to Donald
Houghton, Esq. At the theatre Pauline went ahead
with Nana, and Petrova lagged behind. The moment
they were out of sight, Petrova rushed the letter
across to the doorkeeper, asking him to be sure and
deliver it, but not to say anything about who had
given it to him. He bowed very grandly and said,
'Leave it to me, Miss Fossil.' At that moment Nana
called Petrova, and she had to race up the stairs.

Pauline and Petrova found the evening almost
unbearably long. Each time they came back to the
dressing-room they looked round for a letter, and
there was not one. They came off after their last
entrance and almost cried to find there was still
nothing. Gloomily they peeled off their tights,
and put on their dressing-gowns, and began to
remove their make-up. Then suddenly there was a
knock on the door. Nana opened it. Both Pauline
and Petrova stopped cleaning their faces and
listened.

'Yes,' they heard Nana say. 'What is it?'

'Do Pauline and Petrova Fossil dress here?' a man's voice asked.

'They do.' Nana sounded very uncompromising; they knew she thought they had done something wrong, and was going to deny it if she could.

'Well,' the man went on, 'Mr Houghton says, would you bring the young ladies to his room for a minute?'

Cobweb and Moth stopped cleaning their faces.
They stared at Pauline and Petrova.

'Well I never,' said Cobweb.

'What's Oberon want with you?' Moth
asked.

'Button up your dressing-gowns, dears,' Nana
interrupted, 'and come along. We'll be able to tell
these two what he wants when we've found out.'

Oberon was sitting at his dressing-table. He
turned round as the dresser showed them in. He
held out their letter.

'You sent this?'

Pauline nodded.

He smiled at her.

'What makes you think you could play the
Prince of Wales?'

Pauline felt very shy.

'We've been taught to speak Shakespeare.'

'Who by?'

'A Doctor Jakes. You wouldn't know her.'

'She teaches us English,' Petrova added.

'All right, then. If she teaches you to speak
blank verse, let's hear you.' He nodded at Pauline.
'You begin.'

In a dressing-room with your make-up not
properly off is not a good moment to recite a

speech of 'Puck's', but, as usual, Pauline only had to begin and she was 'Puck'. Petrova found the dressing-gown and rather smeared face a great help for the boy in 'Henry the Fifth'. When they had finished, Oberon shook them both, and Nana, by the hand.

'The casting doesn't rest entirely with me,' he said, 'but I'll do what I can; I can't promise more. Good night.'

Back in the dressing-room Moth and Cobweb were waiting.

'Well,' they asked as the door opened, 'what did he want?'

Pauline and Petrova said nothing, as they were afraid to say they had been for parts, as they knew if they did every child in the theatre would be after them tomorrow. Nana came to the rescue.

'They've been talking in the wings as usual,' she said severely. 'And it wasn't a lie either,' she added as the door closed on Moth and Cobweb, 'for I'm yet to hear of the night when you don't talk in the wings. Come on, Petrova, must get you out of the theatre, or I'll have the stage manager after me, and you don't want to have to tell him you're fourteen, Pauline, or you'll be kept till the end of the show, and that'll mean a nice job for someone fetching you home. And when we get on the tube I'd like to hear what all this Prince of Wales business is about.'

4. More about *Ballet Shoes*

NOW WE *come to the end of the book about which children write and ask 'What happened?'*

First I must explain what had *happened. Pauline had acted in a film and had been an instant success. Posy, who showed signs that she might be a great dancer, had sneaked off alone to persuade a Monsieur Manoff, whose Czechoslovakian ballet was visiting London, to see her dance. Petrova, whose eyes were always on the stars, knew there was only one career for her and that was to be a flier.*

In the last scene in the book a film agent is with Sylvia trying to persuade her to bring Pauline to California. Pauline can't make up her mind, even for a lot of money, to break up the family. Posy is still out and no one knows where. Pauline and Petrova are discussing Pauline's film offer when Posy, hysterical with happiness, rushes in to say Manoff will take her as a pupil in his dancing school in Czechoslovakia.

Petrova gasped:

'But, Posy, how do you think Garnie' – which is what the children called Sylvia – 'is going to afford to send you there?'

Posy was past reason.

'She'll have to get the money. I must go. I must.'

That was when Pauline knew the answer.

'You shall go, Posy,' she said, and went back into the other room and told Garnie to sign her contract.

'That's settled,' she said to Posy when she came out. 'I'm going to make an awful lot of money, enough to keep you and Nana in Czechoslovakia as well as Garnie and me in Hollywood.'

Petrova managed not to cry, but she did wonder what was to become of her.

It was then Gum came back. He stamped in expecting to find everything just as he had left it, including three babies in the nursery. Of course the girls soon put him wise.

'I'm going to Hollywood *with* Garnie to be a film star,' Pauline told him.

'And I'm going to Czechoslovia with Nana to train for ballet under Manoff,' Posy said, thumping his good knee.

Gum looked at Petrova.

'That seems to leave you and me. What do you want to do?'

Posy answered for her.

'Flying and motor cars.'

'That suits me,' said Gum. 'Cook and Clara still here?' They told him they were. 'Good,' he said. 'Then they shall look after us. Might hire a car tomorrow, Petrova, and find a house near an aerodrome where you could study.'

I know that all these plans happened, but of course the children who read Ballet Shoes do not. Now I am going to tell a little about the way things turned out for the three girls, and I hope in such a way that those of you who have not read the book are interested.

5. What Happened to Pauline,
Petrova and Posy

THE FIRST to leave were Sylvia and Pauline. In a way, although they all hated to say 'goodbye', it was a relief when Pauline was really off.

'There wouldn't be as much fuss if it was royalty moving,' Posy whispered to Petrova.

The film company was determined that as they intended to make a star of Pauline she should travel like one. A lady from the company arrived and for three days took Pauline shopping. Pauline had never worn outgrown clothes as Petrova and Posy had to do because she was the eldest. But during the years when they were poor while Gum was away she had cheap clothes, even for the first night of her film her frock was made at home by

Nana. Pauline was now fifteen and the lady from the company made sure she was dressed as the most up-to-date teenager to be found anywhere.

Then there were interviews and photographs.

'They wear me out,' said Posy. 'Here's me chosen to join Manoff's ballet company but nobody cares, but because Pauline is going to Hollywood to make a film people from papers come all day long.'

However, at last the day of departure came. It was in May, so Pauline, looking lovely in a tweed travelling coat over a lightweight frock, stepped into a huge hire car. Her wonderful matching luggage all marked 'Pauline Fossil' was packed in by the chauffeur and she and Sylvia rolled away.

Nana had the last word:

'Don't forget. Wool next the skin, dear. Warm climates can be treacherous.'

Posy left next. She and Nana in a taxi with their rather shabby suitcases piled beside the driver. Nobody could cry when Posy left, for she was radiant. They had not far to go, only to Victoria Station to join Monsieur Manoff and his ballet.

The final move was when pantechnicons came to fetch all the contents of the house in the Cromwell Road. When everything was gone

Gum, Petrova, Cook and Clara got into a car and drove to the midlands. There, until the house Gum had bought was ready for them, they stayed in an hotel. Petrova was in a daze of excitement, for near the new house was an aerodrome, and at the aerodrome a man called Nobby Clark who had undertaken to train her to be a mechanic. Already a governess called Miss Potter came daily to give her lessons.

'Can't have you going to a school,' Gum explained. 'You see, I'm used to travelling. Now if you want to you can come too and we'll take the Potter with us.'

Petrova, crooning over the overalls she was to wear when training at the aerodrome, could not imagine ever wanting to go away, but she could understand that Gum might.

'But if he does,' she told Cook and Clara, 'we'll see we know where he is. We don't want him going away for years and leaving us with no money.'

The part for which Pauline had been given her Hollywood contract was the girl in an English book. The girl, who was called Sara, had run away from home when she found out that her father and mother no longer loved each other, so were not going to share a home any more. Sara adored both parents and the thought of living first with one and then with the other was more than she could bear. So she ran away to Europe where she got mixed up with extraordinary events. Of course in the end her father and mother, having found Sara, were so happy that they joined together again.

It is not easy to act in a film, as Pauline had found when she made her first. Then she had only played a small part, now she had the leading part. She was, of course, rehearsed by a coach, but that too was difficult. When Pauline understood why she was to say something in a certain way she could do it, but if she did not understand she would go on asking 'Why?' until she did understand. At first the coach thought Pauline a horrible girl, but later she came to see how her mind worked and then she and Pauline became friends. It was in fact largely due to her coach that Pauline made the enormous success in that first film that she did.

Her film being such a success Sylvia signed, on Pauline's behalf, a long contract. They rented a very nice house with a swimming pool on the lawn and bought a car and hired a chauffeur. 'It all sounds very grand,' Sylvia wrote to Petrova, 'but for Hollywood we live very simply.'

Two things Pauline insisted on. She must have a private governess. She would not go to the studio school and every eighteen months she must have time off to visit England and Czechoslovakia.

'After all,' she told Mr Silas B. Shoppenhanger, who owned the film company. 'I have two sisters and I must see them. We're family.'

Meanwhile in the midlands Petrova too was a success. She had taken examinations in mechanics and passed them with ease, and now she was promoted to studying aeroplane engines.

'You see,' she explained to Nobby on her fourteenth birthday, 'I want, as soon as I can, to get my pilot's licence. Then, the moment I am eighteen, I can fly alone.'

To Gum she said:

'You wait until I'm grown up – then, if you can buy a little aeroplane, I can fly you anywhere in the world you want to go. And we can visit Czechoslovakia and Hollywood on the way.'

Posy was superbly happy training under Manoff, which well she might be, for Manoff thought her a genius and did not hide how he felt.

'Posy,' he would say, 'soon I am taking this company to America. Before that happens you will be dancing for me. I plan two new ballets written specially for you.'

One plan came true. Pauline took a three months' break and did visit both Petrova and Gum and Nana and Posy. This was a great success. Pauline seemed unchanged. She always had been the star performer in the family and of course the eldest, and she still was. Cook and Clara were a bit in awe of her to start with, but they soon got over it when they found she still liked to come into the kitchen and sit on the table and talk to them.

Posy was charmed to see both Sylvia and Pauline again, but with her dancing was all her life. But Nana was thrilled to see them.

'Oh dear, Miss Sylvia, you wouldn't believe how I've counted the days until you came. Of course I'm glad Posy is doing so nicely at the dancing, but such a language they talk here. And the food! You wouldn't believe the trouble I have to get the simplest things, like oatmeal for porridge and treacle for puddings.'

Sylvia, listening, could see life was hard on Nana. She knew not a word of the language and made no effort to learn. What with school and dancing classes Posy was out all day. It must be a lonely life.

She thought things over and made a suggestion.

'I tell you what we'll do, Nana. We'll change places. You go back to Hollywood with Pauline and I'll stay here and look after Posy. We might at least try it out.'

That was what happened and it was a great success. It was also very fortunate, for the next year the war started, which began in 1939.

To take a huge ballet company plus stage staff, wardrobe and scenery across the world takes immense organization at any time, but during a war it is a nightmare. Transport was hard to arrange and the company moved in isolated groups. Nana, without a word of the language, would have found things terribly difficult, but Sylvia took it in her stride and somehow arrived safely in New York with a wildly excited Posy.

For many of the ballet company life was to be very hard, for the war lasted five years and of course no theatre wanted to engage the company for that long. But Posy never suffered: when, having made a huge success in the new ballets, the company divided into small groups and went on tour, she and Sylvia went to stay with Pauline until the next ballet season started in New York.

As soon as she was old enough Petrova joined a flying service which transported new aeroplanes from the factory where they had been built to the air base which was waiting for them.

'I am so lucky,' she would say to Gum. 'I could so easily have been born at a time when girls didn't fly.'

When they were children living in the Cromwell Road the girls had made a vow on their birthdays. It was: 'We three Fossils vow to try and put our name in history books because it's our own and nobody can say it's because of our grandfathers.'

I don't know if the Fossils ever got their name in history books. Pauline certainly didn't – film stars don't. Posy would for ever be part of ballet history, but not I think ordinary history. Petrova? I don't know, but I sometimes wonder.

6. My Christmas Holidays

I *wonder which is the best of the school holidays. When I was your age I looked forward passionately to all three, but then I hated being at school. Oh, the joy of the last day of term! The moment when you cleared out your desk and dusted all the books, which we had to do, something, which I dare say you don't. Oh, the pleasure of stuffing all the bumph – drawings, essays your parents were supposed to enjoy reading – into your satchel, then shouting goodbyes, striding off for home. For me the striding was in the company of my sisters – one older than myself, one younger. For me – not for my sisters – there was a snag before joy could be unconfined. It was THE ENVELOPE. It lay*

*white and crisp on top of the bumph in my
satchel and without doubt was the bearer of
bad news. It might just as well have had a black
border.*

*Why is it – and this seems to have happened in
all generations – that while the rest of the children
in a family do well at school, one is a complete
failure? It doesn't seem to have anything to do
with brains, more often it would appear to be
sheer cussedness.*

*Picture me and my two sisters coming home for
the start of the Christmas holidays. My sisters,
radiantly happy – and why not? – for in their
envelopes there would be no 'inattentive' or
'slovenly work' nor even 'could do better if she
would try'. They had each a whole column of
'much improved', 'excellent' or 'shows real talent'.*

*Term after term I would loiter by every drain
longing to post my report down it, but I was
always prevented by one of my sisters saying: 'It
will do no good for if you haven't got it Daddy
will suppose it's worse than it is.' Which was not
true for no one could imagine my report worse
than it was.*

*One Christmas holiday my report was so bad
that it actually made my mother laugh. It was the*

result of an exam in which I got two out of a hundred. Surprised, I said without thinking, 'I wonder what I got two for?'

Fortunately the report reading took place the moment we got home. Usually this was followed for me by a 'talk' in Father's study. It was not of course a talk, it was a lecture which combined explaining to me what grief my bad work brought, not only to my school, to my parents but also to God. Father was a parson so I accepted this last as a matter of course, though marvelling why someone as busy as God should have time to grieve because of my bad report.

Then suddenly my talk was over, reports were forgotten and we fell head over heels into the magic of Christmas.

Tennis Shoes

The Heath children have tennis running
through their blood – their father and grandfather
before them were top players – and the twins are
championship material. But tennis isn't the
most important thing in their lives.
Find out what happens when the children take part
in a tennis tournament *and* in the Christmas panto.

7. Acting 'Cinderella'

THE CHRISTMAS of that year Jim and Susan played in their club tournament. They had no chance as it was open and drew first class children from all over the country. It started on the Monday after Christmas and went on for a week. This, they thought, was a splendid week to have a tournament in, as it prevented that 'nothing-nice-will-ever-happen-again' feeling on Christmas night. The twins entered for the singles and the mixed doubles.

The tennis tournament was not the only thing of importance happening that holiday. There was as well to be a play in aid of the hospital. They were all acting. It was *Cinderella*, and rehearsals began immediately after Christmas. The twins felt very important when they explained that during the tournament week they could not promise to come to rehearsals until after six o'clock. They spoke as if they expected to remain in for round after round. Actually, of course, they were not likely to get through one round.

Nicky was jealous about the tournament.

'It's mean, you know, all the things you two get. First the club, and now playing in the tournament. I don't ever seem to get anything at all.'

'But you will,' Jim argued. 'When I'm out working you'll still be lolling about at school and playing at the club. If it comes to that, it must seem very mean to David too. He's got longer to wait than you have.'

David looked up from a new section of farm that he had for Christmas.

'I'm perfec'ly sa'sfied.'

Nicky picked up one of his cows and turned it over.

'Then you shouldn't be. We haven't even got as good parts in the play as they have. I can't see why Susan had to be Cinderella as well as play in a tournament.'

'Well, you couldn't expect to be it yourself,' Jim pointed out. 'You haven't got the hair for it.'

Nicky looked sadly at Susan's plaits. It was an odd world. What luck Susan had! Fancy being born with hair that made it perfectly certain that you would play Cinderella.

'As a matter of fact,' Susan told her, 'I think I would rather be the court jester. Besides, you're going to do juggling. People will think that awfully clever, not knowing about Annie.'

'Ac'ually the best thing is me,' said David. 'I have two songs to sing.'

Susan looked at him in despair.

'Isn't he awful? I don't know how anyone can be as conceited as you, David.'

Nicky squatted down beside the farm. She rearranged a whole row of cows. Instead of waiting to be milked they now looked as if they were going to do a round dance.

'I'm not co'ceited,' David explained. 'I jus' can sing.'

'Because you can do things,' Jim said, 'especially if it's things like singing, you don't want to slop about all over the place telling people about it.'

'I don't slop. I just tell.' David slapped Nicky's hand. 'Will you leave those cows alone. I have to make my milk returns to the Gov'nent. Moving them about upsets them.'

'Don't be mean.' Nicky helped to put the cows back in their proper places. 'I have to play with other people's presents from Daddy and Mummy, because I only get umbrellas.'

'Well, whose fault is that?' Jim pointed out.

Nicky rolled over and picked up Agag's front paws and tried to teach him to dance.

'Mine. I never said it wasn't. Four umbrellas I've had. Next birthday I'm going to ask for something that nobody in the house likes but me, and I'll go and play with it by myself, because you've all been so nasty.'

'We haven't,' Susan objected. 'I've got *Pride and Prejudice*. You wouldn't like that.'

'And I had *Kim*,' said Jim, 'which you wouldn't understand.'

'You never care nothin' for farmin',' David pointed out.

Agag, tried beyond endurance by being forced to dance on his two little back legs, gave a moan. Jim, Susan, and David were very indignant.

'Put him down, Nicky.'

'It's a shame to tease him, poor little fellow.'

'If I was him I'd have bitten you; bein' him, he's too p'lite.'

Nicky patted Agag.

'He doesn't mind a bit, do you, darling?'

Agag never was a dog to bear a grudge. He licked Nicky's face. He had no idea he was letting the others down.

'That dog,' said David in disgust, 'has too f'lict'us a nature.'

Jim clicked his fingers to bring Agag over to him.

'Felicitous, you mean.' He picked up Agag. 'Have you got a felicitous nature, old boy?' Agag yawned. 'He says he doesn't know what felicitous means, and he thinks long words for show are silly.'

David, quite unmoved, went on arranging his farm.

'Agag and me un'erstan's each other.'

Susan and Jim were both knocked out of the singles on the same morning. Susan did not play anything like as well as she could. She was unlucky in that she drew against one of the best players. She did not mind being knocked out by her, but she did dislike the gallery she collected. She felt sure everybody was saying what a bore it was for a good player to have to waste her time playing against her.

Jim played quite well. He had spent most of the summer term and the early part of the autumn term in training for swimming contests. He really showed signs of being quite exceptional. As soon as the swimming season was over he had done what he could to work at his tennis. He practised against a wall whenever he got a chance, and played what squash he could. He took two games in one set, and one in the other, off a boy of sixteen.

Nicky came and watched them play in the doubles. Jim and Susan did what they could to prevent her being brought, but she pleaded to be allowed to watch, and Dr Heath said, as long as she behaved herself, he could not see why not. Neither Jim nor Susan had the slightest hope that she would behave herself. She sat beside her father in the front of the gallery.

'Look at Nicky,' said Susan gloomily to Jim, as they came on to the court. 'I do hope she won't call out anything.'

As a matter of fact Nicky behaved perfectly. She made no remark about the game at all. It was not a bad match. The twins were up against a pair very little older than themselves, and if Jim had been playing as well as he had in the singles, they might have won. He was very anxious not to let Susan down and so went back to his old trick of attempting a killing service. Unfortunately he hardly ever got it over, nor always the miserable little tap that followed as a second ball. He served fault after fault.

'I'm so sorry, Sukie,' he whispered.

'Don't bother,' she whispered back. 'Why don't you do that other service? You got very good at that.'

Even in the middle of the match Jim could not resist an argument.

'I can do this all right really. I don't know what's wrong with it today.'

Susan did not say anything more. She had to get ready to take a service. In any case, she never argued with Jim. It was a waste of time.

After the match was over they went to the changing rooms and had a shower, and then came up and joined their father and Nicky. Nicky looked up at them.

'Well tried, dears.'

Jim could have hit her.

'Thank you. We don't want any criticism from you.'

'A pity,' said Nicky. 'You should listen to Miss Nicky Heath. She could help you a lot.'

'Oh, shut up, Nicky!' Susan whispered. She looked round anxiously to see if anyone could hear.

Dr Heath pulled Susan down beside him.

'Not bad, old lady. On the whole I was pleased with you. You're becoming quite a stylist anyway.'

Jim felt that this praise for Susan was really intended as a criticism of the way he had mucked up his service.

'That service of mine,' he said truculently, 'comes off nine times out of ten.'

Nicky grinned.

'Sad it was ten all day today. Must be Christmas.'

'Oh, shut up!'

'Yes, shut up, Nicky,' Dr Heath agreed. 'Jim doesn't need you or anybody else to tell him he messed up his service. He knows it for himself.'

Jim would have liked to argue. It was not altogether his fault. Even the best players found their service go wrong sometimes. But he felt he was beaten this time. It was true he had mucked the thing up. He was very sick with himself for doing it. Only there were days when it did come off. He could not help trying it just in case. It would be grand to serve like that in your club with everybody watching.

'Do you want to go,' Dr Heath asked, 'or shall we watch for a bit?'

At that moment the game below finished and two more pairs came out. Susan looked down at them.

'Let's watch,' she whispered. 'They are supposed to be frightfully good. Someone told me that the two on the other side might win.'

The game began. It was very fast. Jim and Susan watched in impressed, if now and again critical, silence. Nicky hung over the edge of the gallery, enormously interested. Suddenly she turned to her father.

'That girl' – she pointed at one of the players – 'is very weak on her backhand, isn't she?'

Jim and Susan turned scarlet. They looked round to be sure no one was listening. They were afraid they might be asked to resign from the club if the people heard Nicky being so rude. Fortunately no one was within earshot. Dr Heath pulled Nicky back into her seat.

'You've no right to criticize out loud like that. If anyone is going to complain it would be her partner.'

'But she is weak on her backhand,' Nicky argued. 'You said it was a thing that nobody who played well would ever be.'

'Well, neither would they,' her father whispered.

Nicky's voice grew louder as she argued.

'Do you mean those girls don't play well?' she said clearly.

Jim and Susan were in agony. Jim pinched Nicky's arm.

'Do shut up, Nicky. I'm sure they can hear. You might think of us. We shall look awful.'

'Well, I want to know.' Nicky's voice was louder than ever. 'If good players are good at backhands and that girl isn't good at backhands, then she isn't a good player, and Susan said she was.'

Susan looked imploringly at her father.

'Do make her stop. I'm sure they can hear.'

Dr Heath turned to Nicky. He spoke very severely.

'One more word, and you'll go out and sit in the car until we are ready to go home.'

Nicky closed her lips tight. She thought they were all against her as usual. She leant forward to watch the game, but she had the parting word.

'She doesn't play well,' she hissed at the twins.

Because of Nicky's bad behaviour she was not allowed to come and watch the finals on Saturday. She was very angry, because she enjoyed watching tennis. Besides, she considered that she had been right. Anyway, she had a perfect right to criticize. She thought it most unfair that she should be punished.

The twins went with their father and enjoyed every minute of the games. The day was made particularly exciting for Susan. They were sitting watching when Dr Heath was tapped on the shoulder. He looked round. It was a man who wrote about tennis for one of the papers. He had been up at Cambridge with Dr Heath.

'Edward Heath, isn't it?' he said. Dr Heath nodded. The man looked at Jim and Susan. 'I had no idea these couple of red-heads were yours.'

'I've two more even redder at home.'

The man pulled one of Susan's plaits.

'How old is this lady?'

'Eleven and a half.'

The man turned to Susan.

'You like the game, don't you? I saw you play your singles.' He looked back again at Dr Heath. 'I rather think you've a chip of the old block here. My word, you were a tiger at the game.' He nodded at Susan. 'You ought to have her coached.'

Dr Heath sighed.

'I've rather a large family. I'm coaching them all myself at present. Later on I think their grandfather means to give them some lessons.'

'Good.' The man got up. 'Well, I must go and make some notes for my paper. Hope to see some of your red-heads at Wimbledon in the future. Feel quite hopeful of this lady.'

When he had gone Dr Heath smiled at Susan.

'How's that, Sukey? That's Jeffrey Miller. He writes about tennis. He is supposed to be one of the greatest experts living. You heard him say that he thought you were promising. That's a lot from him.'

Susan was so pleased that she had a lump in her throat. She did not answer. She just gave her father a look, which she knew he knew meant that she was most awfully pleased. The only flaw in being praised like that was that Jim was left out. She did wish it was the doubles that Mr Miller had seen, then they would have been praised together, which would have been so much nicer.

It was a good thing for the twins that they had the play rehearsals to go to for the rest of the holidays, because otherwise they would have felt flat after the tournament was over. *Cinderella* was a grand performance in a hall that had proper lighting. Footlights, and battens of lights overhead, and spotlights to throw on people. Best of all, the lights changed colour, so that really fine effects could be got.

Susan was not honestly a very good actress. She moved beautifully in the ordinary way, but she got awkward on the stage. Of course, with rehearsals, she got used to people watching and she knew it would be easier when she was dressed up, but all the same she was a little angular.

Jim was the prince. He was rather good. He enjoyed the whole thing, except dancing in the minuet at the court ball.

Nicky was one of the people brought in as extra turns at the court ball. She was the jester. She had a lot of knocking people over the head with balloons to do. As well, she did her juggling with two balls. Annie worked very hard to teach her to use three before the first night. It was no good. She always dropped the third ball. So she had to go on using two. She thought it looked more clever to have two balls that were always in the air than use three when one was likely to be on the floor.

David was the page who brought round the shoe the morning after the ball. He had a better part than that sounds because of his songs. There were not any songs in his part really, but two were put in. He sang 'Cherry Ripe' in one act and 'Matthew, Mark, Luke, and John' in the other. They were not really very suitable songs for a page, but they were songs which he could sing well, and everybody thought that more important.

Everybody came to see the play, including Grandfather, who came to stay especially for it. It was a night of triumph for them all. Actually the most successful people were the ugly sisters and the two men who made up a horse, and, of course, the Heaths were not lucky enough to get those parts. But everybody was very proud of them.

Susan looked quite lovely as Cinderella. She wore brown rags at the beginning, which suited her long red hair. In the ballroom scene they had borrowed a ballet frock for her. It was the long kind that came down to the ankles. It was an easy dress for a transformation scene. A lot of fairies came on with the fairy godmother and they danced in front of her, hiding her from the audience, while the fairy godmother buttoned her up. She looked so nice in her ballet frock that when the fairies moved away, and the audience saw her, there was a burst of applause.

Jim was a surprise to everybody. He was a quite nice-looking boy, but nobody had thought very

much about his face. Now, as Prince Charming, in a satin suit and a white wig, he looked really handsome. Everybody said: 'How good-looking those Heath twins are,' which made Dr and Mrs Heath feel very proud.

Nicky's odd-looking face was suited to her jester dress. She looked very small, and when she juggled with her two balls she got a tremendous round of applause.

One of the successes of the evening was David. He got an encore for both his songs. He was almost as popular as the ugly sisters and the two halves of the horse, and that was saying a great deal. The worst of David was that he was not at all surprised. He expected an encore, and would have been very hurt if he had not got it.

After the play was over somebody came on the stage and said that a hundred and twenty-three pounds had been made for the hospital, which was very good indeed. When they got home Grandfather gave them each a wristwatch, because they had done so well. It really was a most exciting evening.

The next night, so that they would not feel too depressed, Grandfather took them all to see the pantomime of *Cinderella*. They had seats in the front row of the dress circle. It, too, was a very nice evening. Taking the matter all round, they thought that their performance of *Cinderella* was the better of the two.

'We did stick much more to the story,' said Susan in the first interval.

'You looked much prettier than that lady,' David observed.

Grandfather opened a box of chocolates.

'I must say I preferred Susan meself.'

'I can't think why they have to have that big fat girl for Prince Charming,' Nicky complained. 'I suppose at Christmas all the men actors are busy, so that they had to dress her up and pretend.'

They were most surprised by the time they reached the next interval. They had never been to a pantomime before, because they had missed the one they had meant to go to, by having measles. They never knew that in pantomimes it is the custom to dash about all over the world. So they were very startled when Cinderella, the two ugly sisters, and Cinderella's mother, who was dressed as an old lady with elastic-sided boots, all came to stay at a smart hotel in Mars. Everybody went to Mars in balloons. There was a very funny scene in a balloon and a very exciting one, of rows of balloons flying across the backcloth. All the same, nobody felt that Mars was the right place for Cinderella to be in. They had to admit that the transformation scene was better done. There were twelve real ponies and a gold coach and proper coachmen, though even then they thought Susan would look much nicer inside the coach than the other Cinderella. The end of the play was better than theirs. All the people that had been to the court ball came marching down a silver staircase. Jim hardly noticed the end of the play, because he was wondering so hard if it were possible to put up a staircase like that in their theatre for next Christmas. They drove home quite dazed with so much dancing and singing and lights.

'Thank you so much, Grandfather,' said Susan. 'It was lovely.'

'Yes, it was,' Jim agreed. ''Though I think they ought to stick more to the story.'

'Don't you think, Grandfather' – Nicky snuggled against him – 'there ought to have been a jester in the court scene, like me?'

David leant against Grandfather's other side.

'It was all mos' sumt'us,' he murmured, and went to sleep.

8. Preparing for Christmas

*C*HRISTMAS DIDN'T *begin as early when I was a child as it does now. Shops did not start to decorate before December and you never saw a Father Christmas until about two weeks before Christmas when, as now, you could meet him in toy shops where – in those days – for sixpence you could shake him by the hand and get a present. But of course it was what went on at home which made us feel Christmassy.*

The first Christmas thing we had to do was make the Christmas decorations, they were never bought in shops in those days. We three girls and my brother would sit round the table in what we still called 'the nursery'. In the middle of the table was a large bowl of homemade paste and we each had a brush and a packet of brightly coloured tissue paper strips which we, by hooking them through each other, turned into chains. You very seldom see paper-chains now, so many pretty things are on the market to take their place. But I can promise you – and any of you who have made them will back me up – there is nothing so full of the spirit of Christmas as making paper-chains.

Of course the moment the chains were made they had to be hung up. This I think must have been done by the grown-ups, for I don't remember being allowed up a ladder which was necessary and which I would have enjoyed.

I don't think paper-chains went beyond the nursery for downstairs we trimmed everything that was trimmable with holly. Holly was on everything: lights, pictures, clocks, ornaments – it must have driven those who dusted mad before Christmas was over. In the middle of the hall there was a light to which a big bunch of holly and a few sprigs of mistletoe were attached. The mistletoe was put in the bunch surreptitiously by my mother, who thought it looked pretty. My father did not believe in putting up mistletoe because it might turn minds to kissing. But whose minds? We three little girls were too young to have thought of such *a thing and who was there to kiss? Only the curate and who would want to kiss him? Perhaps Father thought of visitors and those who worked for us. I shall never know but I do know that, thanks to Mother, mistletoe always appeared.*

Theatre Shoes

Every family has its secrets but it is a huge
surprise for the three Forbes children to discover
their grandmother was once a famous actress!
Grandmother sends them to stage school, where
they are expected to work hard and follow in the
family footsteps, even at Christmastime.

9. Christmas Day

CHRISTMAS DAY in every family is built up on little bits of custom. Something happens one year and it is amusing and gay and Christmassy, and so it becomes part of all future Christmases. Christmas Day in Guernsey had been full of things like that. The children's father had come into their nursery for the opening of their stockings and there were always band instruments in each stocking, and when the stocking opening was finished they played 'Good King Wenceslas' with their father singing the solo part of the King and Mark singing the page, and a lot of repeat verses for the band only. There had been visits to friends after morning church and a lovely party with a

Christmas tree in somebody else's house in the afternoon.

When the children came to live with Grandfather, Hannah did the best she could with Christmas. She managed the band instruments in the stockings and she tried to sing 'Good King Wenceslas'. This was lucky, because that first Christmas of the war with their father away had felt a bit queer and miserable, but Hannah singing the King's part in 'Good King Wenceslas' was so funny that they all laughed until they felt sick. As Hannah could not sing 'Good King Wenceslas', they made her sing 'The First Noel' as a solo, with the children helping in the Noel bits; and this, having happened for three Christmases, was now an established custom. There were other things that had happened in the vicarage on Christmas Day that had become customs. There was a party in the afternoon in the house of a big family where there was a Christmas tree, and charades were played, and Christmas Day had finished with a special supper of scrambled eggs made by themselves, eaten in the kitchen with Hannah.

This year Christmas was going obviously to be quite different from anything the children had known before. They were keeping, of course, a few of their own customs, but mostly they were going to be part of Grandmother's. Christmas Day was the day when she received her family. She had them all to dinner in the evening. It made the day exciting in a way to be going to meet Aunt Lindsey and Uncle Mose and Uncle Francis and Aunt Marguerite, and to be going to see Miranda and Miriam away from the Academy.

'Proper set-up it is,' said Alice. 'I'm worn to a shred by the time I've laid the Cain and Abel, and when it comes to dishing up I never know how to drag my plates of meat up the apples and pears. This year it won't half be a set-up. We're receiving in style. We've got a part. We're on top of the world. We shan't half see that we're number one at our own party.'

Because of the Fossil scholarships, Sorrel and Holly had a shilling pocket money every week. This, divided into three, made eightpence each. They spent some of their eightpences on their month's sweet ration, and they each gave a penny a week to the Red Cross; and there was, of course, a penny for the collection on Sundays, but what was over they had saved for Christmas presents. They could not buy much because there was nothing much that was cheap to buy; but they managed parcels all round. Sorrel had bought a party hair bow on a slide for Holly, and some pencils for Mark. For Alice there was a calendar with a picture of people about a hundred years ago drinking round an inn on a very snowy day; for Hannah there was also a calendar, but hers had a little wreath of holly and a verse that might have been part of a carol. Mark gave Sorrel and Holly some drawing pins, which seemed a funny present, but was one of the few things he could afford to buy that was useful. For Hannah there was a little wooden ruler, and for Alice some tin-tacks. Holly had never been able to grasp how coupons worked. Up till almost Christmas Day she hoped to buy soap for everybody, because she liked the smell. When at last she realised that it made no difference what shop you went into they would all want soap coupons, it was Christmas Eve and the shops were nearly empty, so in desperation she bought buns, not even nice buns, but the sort you would expect to get when you queue up for them on Christmas Eve. For Grandmother the children had put their money together. They bought a white heath in a little pot. It was really a tiny plant and it cost a fearful lot, but it was the best they could manage; so that was that.

Christmas Day started in a proper way. There were the stockings and there was Hannah.

'Happy Christmas, dear,' she said to Sorrel. 'Don't you touch your stocking now, I'm just popping along to fetch Mark and Holly.'

Holly sat in bed beside Sorrel, and Mark sat the other end, and Hannah sat on the side of the bed. Of course, the stockings had not got in them the good things they used to have because things like that were not in the shops any more. But the fun of Christmas and stockings and presents is obviously not in what the presents are made of, for though the trumpets were cardboard instead of tin, and the drum was only paper and the triangle was very small, and the mouth organ only had four notes, it was all the funnier trying to be an orchestra with them.

Alice came as audience.

'Happy Christmas, everybody. I thought I better hear old Hannah sing her carol. I was afraid if I wasn't here to shout to the neighbours we might have the police in.'

It was a very nice carol singing, and when Hannah got to the bit:

They looked up and saw a Star
Shining in the East beyond them far.
And to the earth it gave great light,
And so it continued by day and by night,

it was as much Christmas Day as ever it had been. Alice wiped her eyes.

'Christmas carols always make me cry, and that's a fact.' She laid four little parcels on the bed. 'You pay your money and you take your choice.'

How Alice had managed to save the sugar and get the treacle off the points, nobody knew and nobody asked; but there were four packets of toffee, home-made, brown and stiff. There were no sweets in the stockings this year and Christmas Day cannot be said properly to have begun without that sickish feeling that comes from eating sweets before breakfast; so the hat was, as it were, put on the day when they all had a piece of Alice's toffee in their mouths.

Hannah's church was very nicely decorated. There was not much holly, but the decorators had done very well with evergreens and red berries from other plants wired on to look like holly berries. In an alcove there was a beautiful crib, with stars shining through the back of the stable and the Virgin Mary sitting by the manger with the Baby on her knee, and two sheep and a donkey and four cows kneeling in the straw, looking reverent. The hymns met with everybody's approval. They began with 'Hark, the herald angels,' and they sang 'While shepherds watched' during the collection, and 'God rest you merry, gentlemen,' as they went out.

'Just what we might have had at home,' said Hannah. 'I can't praise higher.'

In the afternoon it was not a bad day, so the children went over to the Square garden; and there, on the grass, were two boys and a girl kicking about a football. Evidently, what the head gardener had said was true. Now that the chance of bombing was less, the children were beginning to come back. Holly and the smaller boy, whose name was Robert, went off to ride on his tricycle that he had been given that morning, and Sorrel and Mark played football with the other two children. They got very hot and the time passed extraordinarily quickly, and they were amazed when the nurse belonging to the other children came along and said it was nearly time for tea.

Sorrel did wish she had got something nice to wear. She had her school velvet, but it had been outgrown before Grandfather died, and she had been meant to have another as soon as the coupons would run to it. Although she did not seem to have grown very much, the frock seemed to fit her a great deal worse since she last wore it. She seemed to have got broader. It was difficult to get it to fasten at the back, and when it was fastened it made her feel short of breath. It had luckily got short sleeves, but they seemed disobliging and cut into her arms. It was not so terribly wrong in length, she had thin legs and a short frock did not matter. As well as fitting badly, it was shabby looking. It had thin places where there hardly seemed to be velvet any more, but only the stuff that velvet is made on, and it had lost its colour in places. It was meant to be green, but Sorrel noticed as she put it on that in quite a lot of spots it was much nearer grey. 'If only this wasn't the first time that the uncles and aunts are seeing me!' Sorrel thought. 'They're bound to expect rather a lot from Mother's child, and really, I do look pretty drab. I do hope Holly and Mark will make a better impression. It wouldn't be so bad if only I could put my bad clothes down to the war; but Miranda and Miriam live in the war too, and I bet they look quite nice.'

Mark was looking ordinary except that he was unusually well brushed and clean. He wore his grey shorts, a white shirt and his school tie. Alice had said that she thought he should wear white socks and that Grandmother would expect it. Luckily, Mark had not heard this suggestion and Hannah treated it with scorn.

'I know what's right for Mr Bill's children, and that's how things are going to be.'

Holly looked rather nice. She was at the right age for party clothes, and with her curls she was the party-frock sort. She had, of course, got all the clothes Sorrel used to have and had now outgrown. She was wearing a white crêpe de Chine frock, and the little cherry-coloured bow that was Sorrel's present in her hair. Hannah would not have said so for the world, but she was very proud of Holly when she had finished with her. Sorrel hoped when she came along for Alice to inspect her that perhaps she did not look as bad as she thought she did, but what Alice said was:

'Well, there's a war on and you're at least covered, and I suppose we mustn't expect more.'

Which, the more you thought about it, the less encouraging it was.

To save heating and trouble, dinner was being served at one end of Grandmother's drawing room. The children thought when they were dressed they would go down, but Alice had given her instructions.

'Nobody takes a step till I fetches them. We are more fussy about Christmas Day than anybody would believe. All kinds of goings on we have. You'll see.'

When the children were called down, Alice did not do what she usually did and announce them, but she led them into the drawing room, which they found entirely empty. By the fire was an armchair with Grandmother's green cushion in it. The sliding doors were closed. Alice, who was rushed because of cooking the dinner, gave Sorrel her instructions.

'You stand round your Grandmother's chair until your uncles and aunts arrive, and then you'll do what the rest of the family do, you can't go wrong if you keep your eyes open.'

They longed to ask 'wrong about what?' but Alice had dashed out shouting to Hannah to come and lend her a hand.

Sorrel looked at Mark and Mark looked at Holly; and all of a sudden it seemed so silly standing solemnly in a row round an empty armchair that they began to giggle. Mark giggled so much that he had to lie down on the floor. Then they heard the front door bell. Sorrel pulled him to his feet.

'Oh, goodness! There's the uncles and aunts! Do get up, it's most terribly important that we shouldn't be a disgrace. We don't want them to despise the Forbes.'

A perfectly strange man dressed as a butler threw open the drawing room door and roared out, 'Mr Moses Cohen, Mrs Cohen, Miss Cohen.'

The first person to come in was Miriam. She stood just inside the door, and in a very affected way, that was not a bit like her, said:

'This is my Daddy, and this is my Mummy.' As the children knew quite well that she called her parents Mum and Dad, and as Miriam was never affected, they stared at her in amazement. Miriam saw their faces and added, in a hoarse whisper, 'We always work up everybody's entrance on Christmas Day.'

Aunt Lindsey came in. She was dark and rather severe looking, and very smart. She stood in the doorway with both hands outstretched, and said in an acting sort of voice:

'Little Addie's children!'

She then stood to one side. There was a moment's pause and there was Uncle Mose with a tiny cardboard hat on the side of his head, rubbing his hands in front of him.

'Vell! Vell! Vell!'

Evidently saying 'Vell! Vell! Vell!' like that was something for which he was famous, because as soon as he had finished saying it, Aunt Lindsey and Miriam laughed.

Once the laugh was over and the Cohen family safely in the room, everybody began to behave in an ordinary way. Miriam raced across and hugged her three cousins and said 'Happy Christmas', and told them what she had been given for presents. Aunt Lindsey kissed them and was very nice, and Uncle Mose told them to feel in his pockets, and out came three envelopes marked Sorrel, Mark and Holly, and in each one was a ten-shilling note! He kissed Sorrel and Holly and rubbed Mark's hair the wrong way, and told them what he would like them to do would be to buy a book each, but that the money was their own and they could spend it how they liked. They took a great fancy to Uncle Mose.

The Cohens had no sooner got safely into the drawing room than the Brains arrived. The strange man dressed as a butler said, 'Sir Francis and Lady Brain. Miss Brain.' This time Miranda came in first. She stood in the doorway, and said in her lovely voice:

'A merry Christmas, everybody.' Then she turned and held out both hands, and added in a surprised voice, as if she had not known she was there, 'Mummy!'

Aunt Marguerite was shorter than Aunt Lindsey, and thinner. She had an anxious, strained expression. She put one arm round Miranda.

'A happy Christmas.' And then, holding out her free hand into the passage, 'Look who's here! Come to say merry Christmas to everybody.'

Uncle Francis was a large man with a big, booming deep voice, which sounded as though he kept it mellow by giving it caramels. He looked round the drawing room as if he were surprised to find himself there. He stood between Aunt Marguerite and Miranda, an arm round each.

'My dear wife, my little daughter, this is an occasion.' And then, with a big smile round the room, 'A merry Christmas to you all from the Brain family.'

The moment this introduction was over, Aunt Marguerite ran across the drawing room to hug Aunt Lindsey, but her eyes were on the children.

'Oh, isn't this fun! I have so wanted to meet you, but we've been touring.' She kissed each of the children in turn. 'I didn't know what to bring you, dears; it's so hard these days to find anything nice.' She turned to Miranda. 'Run and get the parcels out of the hall.'

Miranda and Miriam were both looking as well dressed as Sorrel was afraid they would. Miranda had on a party dress of green taffeta, and Miriam was in white with an orange ribbon round the waist. Sorrel felt at her worst, as if she were sticking out in all the wrong places.

Miranda, who had gone into the passage to fetch the parcels, came back with her arms full. Aunt Marguerite selected three of the parcels and handed them to the children.

'Don't undo them until Grandmother comes. We keep the presents until then.'

Grandmother's arrival was announced. The butler threw open the drawing-room door:

'Miss Margaret Shaw.'

Grandmother stood in the open doorway. She was wearing a dress of black trailing chiffon, and fox furs, and her hair was held up on the top of her head with a diamond comb. There was not very much light in the hall and as she stood there she did not look like an old lady, but like somebody out of a fairy story. She stretched out both arms.

'My children! Now this is really Christmas.'

The children that she referred to were, of course, Aunt Lindsey and Aunt Marguerite, and they hurried forward and kissed their mother.

'Darling Mother.'

'Mother dearest.'

Then Uncle Francis came across the room and kissed Grandmother's hand.

'Wonderful, wonderful woman!'

Uncle Mose followed Uncle Francis. He kissed Grandmother's hand, too. All this time Sorrel, Mark and Holly had been waiting to do something, and now they had their cue. Miranda and Miriam danced across the room.

'Granny, Granny!'

Uncle Mose gave a wink and a jerk of his head to Sorrel. She caught hold of Mark and Holly and they hurried forward. After kissing Grandmother, the right thing to do seemed to be to lead her to her chair. She sat down, shook out her skirts, rested her back comfortably against her cushion and twinkled up at Aunt Lindsey.

'Well, what is it this year?'

Aunt Lindsey looked positively nervous as she produced her parcel.

'I do hope it's something you'll like, darling; but you know how difficult things are.'

Aunt Lindsey, being obviously so nervous, seemed to affect everybody else, and they all leaned forward while Grandmother opened the box. Inside was a beautiful handbag.

'Of course,' Sorrel thought, 'one shouldn't criticise one's grandmother,' but she did seem to take presents in a funny way. She turned the bag upside down, she smelt the leather, and she looked at the lining; and it was this that took most of her attention, for when she had examined it carefully she said to Aunt Lindsey in a shocked way:

'Artificial.'

'I know, dear,' Aunt Lindsey agreed, 'but there is so little real silk about these days.'

Uncle Mose gave Grandmother an affectionate tap on the shoulder.

'You've fooled her as usual, Mother. I know you're not looking at the lining; you're hoping to find the price ticket.'

Grandmother twinkled up at him.

'Quite right. I love knowing what things cost.'

Aunt Marguerite laid her present on Grandmother's knee. This time it was a thin parcel. Inside was an umbrella.

'I know, dear,' Aunt Marguerite said, 'that you never have used an umbrella, and that you never walk anywhere; but now that you're going into this show, I do think you ought to be prepared in case you have to, there are so very few taxis.'

Grandmother turned over the umbrella as if it were some curiosity from a foreign country.

'Interesting. I remember I carried one just like this in the first act of *Aunt Celia*. You remember, that was the play when I had to try and look dowdy.'

Uncle Francis cleared his throat.

'Good umbrellas are scarce today, Mother.'

Grandmother answered him in a very good imitation of his own voice.

'Then it was very kind of the Brains to give it to me.' All of a sudden, her manner changed and she swung round in her chair and looked at the children. 'Now, what about the children's parcels? Where are they? Bring them out.'

Aunt Marguerite's parcels were opened. In Sorrel's and Holly's were very pretty strings of beads, and in Mark's a penknife. As well, there was a parcel each from Aunt Lindsey. A book by Ransome for Sorrel, a torch for Mark, and a game for Holly. They took a very good view of their aunts' ideas of presents.

The children had made Grandmother's heath look better by putting round the pot a bow that Alice had found. They had given it to Alice to put on the table. Now Sorrel began rather to wish they had not. Evidently this was the right time to give presents, and anyway it looked pretty shabby of them not to have got presents for at any rate Miranda and Miriam; but even with the presents they had given they were cleaned out.

They need not have worried; their present was a great success. Grandmother said she should put it on her dressing table at the theatre to bring her luck.

Dinner was tremendous fun. Grandmother and Uncle Mose were both terribly funny and always funny about things to do with the children. First, it was about Miranda, and then Sorrel perhaps, and then Mark. It seemed to be that kind of party when nobody minds how excited you get or how noisy you are. There was turkey to eat. Uncle Mose had managed to get it from a friend and he told a long, silly story about how he had led it on a gold ribbon right up from the city. Of course, they all knew it was not true, but they enjoyed it just the same. There was plum pudding of a sort to follow and some mince pies. The children all chose the plum pudding because, as Alice laid it down, she said:

'There's a thimble, a china baby, a horseshoe and a sixpence in there, and I want everything except the sixpence back for next year, so mind you don't swallow them.'

The thimble and the china baby were found by Holly, the horseshoe by Miranda, and Uncle Mose got the sixpence. Uncle Francis had brought with him a bottle of port wine, which he said he had got from his club, and when dinner was over, everybody, including the children, were given some to drink. It was for toasts. There seemed to be a custom about this. First of all, Grandmother's health was drunk, and Uncle Francis made a speech about it. Then Aunt Lindsey fetched an enormous photograph of Uncle Henry and put it down by Grandmother's side, and Grandmother made a speech about 'my eldest boy', and everybody drank to Uncle Henry. Then Grandmother made a speech about the Cohens and another about the Brains. The children, who had not had very much port to begin with, began to wonder how many more healths were going to be drunk, because even though they took only teeny little sips they had not much left, when Grandmother suddenly held up her hand for silence.

'There's someone we specially want to drink to tonight. These children's father. May he be home with them by next Christmas.'

It was quite awful; but somehow, thinking of its being Christmas and even imagining him home by next Christmas was so absolutely gorgeous, it made Sorrel want to cry. She looked at Mark and saw he was going to cry too, and then she looked at Holly and saw that she was, too. Fortunately, Sorrel was not the only one who knew what was going to happen. Uncle Mose was quicker than she was. Before more than two tears had flopped down Sorrel's cheeks and Mark had only got to the making-faces stage, and Holly was just puckering up, he had got off his chair and was walking round the table on his hands.

None of the children had ever seen a person do that before, and they were so interested watching him that the crying moment passed, and they were back feeling Christmassy again.

After dinner they played charades, and the man dressed as a butler, Alice and Hannah came in as audience.

The charades started like ordinary party charades, only of rather a grand kind. Uncle Mose, Grandmother, Miranda, Holly and Aunt Lindsey made a side. They acted 'manifold' but the word did not seem to have much to do with it. It was just thinking of amusing things to give everybody, especially the children, to do. The second charade was acted by the rest of the family. This was more serious because Uncle Francis seemed only to play serious parts, and so that charade was not very funny. It was when they were playing the third charade that Grandmother and Uncle Mose got together.

'You must do Jaques in *As You Like It*,' Uncle Mose urged, 'only, instead of the apple, I've got a prop for you.'

The children had never seen Uncle Francis act. So it was not half as funny to them as it seemed to be to the others.

Grandmother, with an overcoat on to show she was being a man, stood with an enormous carving knife in one hand and peeled a pumpkin. And while the skin fell on the floor she rolled out very slowly the Seven Ages of Man speech. There were immense pauses when she looked up and did things with her eyes, and this simply convulsed Aunt Lindsey, Uncle Mose and Alice. Alice laughed so much that she had to hold her inside, and she kept murmuring to the butler:

'She'll be the death of me.'

Hannah, sitting beside her, never laughed at all. Alice had told her that this was Shakespeare – and Shakespeare, according to what Hannah had heard, was not a thing to laugh at. After that, Uncle Mose pretending to be Aunt Marguerite and Grandmother pretending to be Uncle Francis, did a scene from *Macbeth*. Sorrel, who had learnt *Macbeth*, knew that neither of them was using the real words, but making it up. Some of the things that Uncle Mose did were really funny, but otherwise the people who enjoyed themselves most were Grandmother and Uncle Mose. Uncle Francis was not amused at all.

Then the charades were over. Grandmother went back to her chair and Aunt Lindsey looked at her watch.

'I think it's time we started the carols.'

They sang 'The First Noel' and 'Good King Wenceslas'. And then Grandmother held out a hand to Mark.

'Come here, grandson. I hear from Madame Fidolia that you can sing. What carol will you sing for us?'

Mark did not want to sing at all. It was that sort of party which, as nobody was stern with anybody, had got to the point when knocking other people about, especially grown-ups, was fun. Mark felt more in the mood to stand on his head than to sing a carol, but Grandmother was holding him firmly and she obviously meant to have her way.

'If I sing one you won't say "sing another", will you?'

Grandmother looked round at her daughters.

'See how he bullies me; you'd never have dared do that. Very well, Mark, just one carol and I won't ask for another.'

They had learnt at the Academy, 'I Saw Three Ships'. It was easy to sing without a piano, and Mark liked it. He leant against Grandmother and sang it all through.

There was complete silence when he had finished. Sorrel did not wonder, for, really, Mark's singing was a very nice noise. She looked at him with pride. It was a good thing that one of them could shine in this clever family. Uncle Francis was the first to speak, and he used his most caramel voice:

'Beautiful, beautiful.'

Aunt Lindsey kissed her mother.

'I think that's the right ending to a lovely evening. We've hired a car, you know, and it ought to be here any minute.'

Grandmother was kissing everybody.

'Goodnight, dears. Goodnight, Francis. Goodnight, Marguerite. God bless you all.'

10. Christmas Presents

*L*OOKING BACK *it is strange that that very pretty custom, which comes to us from abroad, of hanging a holly wreath on the front door never existed when I was a child. Certainly we never had one and I do not remember seeing one. Stranger still, we never had a crib in the house. There was one of course in the church, but in those days the charming custom of making a crib for the home never reached us. Today, when so many people give immense imagination and talent to building exquisite cribs which they look at with joy until Twelfth Night, I regret that as a child I never had the chance to build one.*

I don't know about you, but I plan to have a little lit crib in my home next Christmas.

Before Christmas there never seem enough hours in the day to get through all you have to do. First on the list of course is shopping. All my life I have tried to get ahead with my Christmas shopping, but I have never succeeded. I make careful lists months beforehand and by October I have started to shop, but I never catch up with my own tail. You know how it is – something somebody wants which you could have bought anywhere a month or so ago suddenly disappears. In London, where I live, this means travelling miles from one shopping area to another wearing out both the feet and the temper. I suppose if you live in the country it's worse for it means going from one town or village to another. It's worth the effort though if you run what you want to earth. You feel as if you had won an Olympic Gold Medal, and when you see the face of the person you give it to all your labour is worthwhile. 'Oh, bless you! It's what I most wanted and I was scared stiff nobody would give it to me.'

I got my first watch off the Christmas tree, and you know what a first watch means. I must have *been about eleven. You would laugh if you saw it today, it was made of what was called gunmetal fastened onto me by a metal bow attached to a pin. A watch like that was all the rage in those days, just as much in fashion as the latest craze in watches is today. I forget who gave mine to me, but I do know however much of a search the giver had to find it, he or she must have thought every second worthwhile if they saw my face when I opened the box in which it arrived. In fact even now, all those years later, if I flag in my search for a special present I see again my little gunmetal watch and I plod on.*

How easy it was when one was tiny. My brother when he was just four gave everybody who had to have a present a sugar mouse. Sugar mice complete with pink noses and wool tails in those far-off days cost one halfpenny each. The only person who did not get a mouse was me. When I asked my brother why he said: 'I only had four pennies which is eight mice, with you it would have been nine. I like you least so I left you out.' Even at just four I thought that showed a poor Christmas spirit.

Present buying is only half the business of present giving. Thank goodness, when I was a child there was none of the elaborate parcel doing up there is today. It was plain brown paper and string with perhaps a piece of holly stuck in the string. How children manage today with elaborate paper, ribbons, bows and sticky tape I can't imagine. They must be exhausted by Christmas Day.

Circus Shoes

When their Aunt Rebecca dies, Peter and
Santa face the awful prospect of life in
separate orphanages – until they find a
Christmas card from their only living
relative, Uncle Gus, who works in a circus.

11. The Christmas Card

PETER and Santa felt miserable. In their way they missed Aunt Rebecca. But they missed her for odd, funny things, and they both knew how the other was feeling so there was no need to keep talking about it. Inside, though they did not talk about that either, they were both worrying. After all they were not babies, they knew what happened to annuities when people died, and though, of course, they also knew that somebody or other is bound to look after children, it might not be the sort of looking after anyone would care for.

The worst of it was there had to be a time of hanging about. The moment Aunt Rebecca died Mr Stibbings wrote to the duchess's executors, explaining what had happened, and about Peter and Santa, and asking if something could be done until they were old enough to earn their own livings. Meanwhile it was decided, if the executors said no, then they were to go to an orphanage.

The letter came a week after Aunt Rebecca died. It arrived at teatime. Mrs Ford, Madame Tranchot, and Miss Fane were all there, but no one liked to open the letter because it was, of course, addressed to Mr Stibbings. It was put on the mantelpiece and they all stared at it. Peter and Santa could not eat any more tea because they wanted so badly to know what it said, which was a pity because there was some particularly good hot buttered toast.

'Do you think,' Peter suggested, 'that I had better take it round to him?'

Mrs Ford looked at Madame Tranchot, who looked at Miss Fane. All their faces said the same thing: 'Don't let him do that because I want to know what is in it.' But none of them liked to say quite that. Mrs Ford got round the difficulty by starting to cry.

'It does seem hard that what concerns the nephew and niece of my oldest friend' – here she gave a big sniff – 'should be discussed behind my back.'

Peter kicked Santa under the table. She saw he was angry and embarrassed about the crying and might be rude. She thought quickly.

'How would it be if Peter and I went round and told him it was here?'

Everybody thought that a good idea. So Peter and Santa, without giving anyone a chance to change their minds, rushed out. Outside Mr Stibbings's house they stood still a moment.

Santa panted, for they had run all the way:

'I feel awful inside. Do you?'

Peter nodded.

'Like waiting at the dentist's. I wish we knew what it said. Just suppose it's an orphanage.'

Luckily Mr Stibbings was in and said he would come at once. But Mr Stibbings's 'at once' was almost as slow as other people's 'presently.' Although it was April and not a bit cold, it was astounding how he fussed before he would go out. It was nearly five minutes before he found his scarf, though Peter and Santa helped look, as well as Mr Stibbings's housekeeper. In the end the housekeeper remembered he had worn it in bed one night, and she ran upstairs and found it tied in a black wool bow to one of the bed knobs. When all the scarf (and it was a very long one) was wound round Mr Stibbings, Peter held out the overcoat.

'Here you are, sir.'

Mr Stibbings looked over his glasses in a hurt way.

'All right, my boy. All in good time. Speed is the curse of the age.'

Peter looked so much as if he was going to say something which might sound rude, and, anyway, Santa knew that Mr Stibbings was the sort of man whom hurrying made slow, so she broke in. She asked about an ostrich egg on the hall table. It did what she wanted, in that it stopped Peter speaking or Mr Stibbings feeling annoyed at being rushed, but it took six minutes before they got away from ostriches, and Mr Stibbings dressed and out of the front door.

'You are a fool,' Peter whispered. 'Fancy asking about that then.'

Santa did not answer, because she knew Peter knew why she had done it, and that, in a way, he thought it a good idea. It came natural to him to answer back and it never helped in the end.

When they got back to the house Mr Stibbings opened the letter. He opened it very slowly, because whatever he did he was slow at. Then he put his spectacles straight. Then he did what the children thought an awfully mean thing. He read the letter to himself. Peter turned red and looked so angry that Santa slipped round to him and whispered: 'Don't ask what's in it, because they will.' She jerked her head at the three women at the table.

She was quite right; even before the letter was finished Mrs Ford was crying. Directly Mr Stibbings stopped reading she said in a choked voice: 'That I should live to see the day when what concerns the welfare of the nephew and niece of my oldest friend was kept from me!'

Luckily Mr Stibbings hated crying as much as Peter and Santa did. He made the sort of cough people make when they are looking for the right words. Then he turned to the children.

'My dear young people, I fear it is not good news. It seems that all the money the duchess left is held in trust for a grandson who is a minor. He is . . .' He opened the letter again and started to look through it; but before he found the name Peter broke in:

'I know. It's that Lord Bronedin.'

Mr Stibbings looked up, surprised.

'That's quite right. The name is Lord Bronedin. You know of him?'

Peter and Santa made each other a very understanding face. Then Peter said:

'I'd just about say we do.'

Mr Stibbings was too interested in other things to ask them what they meant; instead he sat down in the armchair and looked like people look when they know nobody is going to like what they have to say. He rearranged his spectacles to a better position on his nose, put the tips of his fingers together, then looked at the children.

'I was afraid that this was the reply we should receive. But thanks to those whom I may call your good friends' – he turned to the three women – 'other arrangements are in train. We have arranged for you, Peter, dear boy, at Saint Bernard's Home for Boys. You, Santa, are going to Saint Winifred's Orphanage.'

'What!'

Santa was so startled that the word came out in a shout. 'We aren't going together?'

Mrs Ford made clicking sounds with her tongue.

'Don't shout, dear. There are different homes for boys and girls.'

Santa turned on her.

'Not always there aren't.'

'Grammar! Grammar!' Mrs Ford wagged her finger at her. Then she took out her handkerchief and wiped her eyes. 'This is not the arrangement I wished for –'

Santa was so upset she felt she would scream if she had to hear about being the niece and nephew of her oldest friend again. So she interrupted:

'If you don't like the arrangement, don't let it happen. It needn't. There must be somewhere we could go together if only you looked for it.' She came to Mrs Ford and shook her arm to be sure she was listening. 'Peter and I couldn't live in two different places, you must see that.'

Miss Fane leant across the table. She held out her hand, plam upwards, as if she expected Santa to put her hand into it.

'I understand how you feel, little one. Separation is terribly hard. But, believe me, your violin will help.'

Santa stamped her foot. She sobbed while she spoke:

'How can you say that? Why should it make it better if I played "Art thou weary?" six hundred times a day?' She turned desperately to them all. 'You must find a place for us. Here you sit, and all you say is it can't be helped. But it's got to be helped. I won't live somewhere else than Peter. And he wouldn't either. Would you, Peter?'

They all looked at Peter. He was leaning against the mantelpiece. His hands were in his pockets and he was staring at the floor, not seeming interested in what was going on. Santa could not see him clearly because she was crying so hard that everything was out of focus. But she felt a cold feeling inside. Peter was not going to fight. Ordinarily he was so much more quickly angry than she was that if he were going to be angry he would have been by now. Mr Stibbings looked at him with approval.

'Peter is sensible, Santa. He knows what must be must be.'

Peter looked up. He came over to the table and stood beside Santa.

'That's right, sir.' As he spoke he dug his elbow into Santa's side. If ever a dig in the ribs meant 'Don't be a fool, trust me', that one did. He turned to Mrs Ford: 'I shouldn't worry. I expect it won't be bad at Saint Bernard's Home for Boys and

Santa will get used to Saint Winifred's Orphanage. Won't you, Santa?

After the dig in the ribs Santa felt better, and she knew from the way he said she would get used to the orphanage that he had a plan, and she guessed it would help if she seemed to cheer up. She dried her eyes.

'No. I suppose it will be all right. It was just I was so surprised. I had never thought of us not going together.' As she said this she could not help a wobble in her voice. She was sure Peter meant to do something, but after all they were only children, and probably police and people like that would be on the side of Mr Stibbings, Mrs Ford, Madame Tranchot, Miss Fane, Saint Bernard's, and Saint Winifred's. She tried to look brave, but she did not feel it.

Peter pulled two chairs up to the table. He pushed Santa into one and he sat on the other.

'There's just one or two things, sir. When do we go?'

Mr Stibbings looked at Mrs Ford, Mrs Ford looked at Madame Tranchot, Madame Tranchot looked at Miss Fane. They all looked embarrassed. Mr Stibbings cleared his throat.

'I'm afraid, dear boy, it will have to be tomorrow. Your lamented aunt only left a few pounds in ready money. That is exhausted. We are all poor people or –'

'I know,' Peter broke in. 'You've all been awfully kind.' He paused a moment. Then he said firmly: 'My aunt left some jewellery and stuff. If we are going tomorrow Santa and I would like it tonight.'

Mr Stibbings was a stupid man in a lot of ways, but he meant to be kind. He was very worried at what Peter asked. The duchess had given Aunt Rebecca quite a lot of bits of jewellery, many of them not very beautiful, but all of them good in their way. But should the children be trusted with them? Besides which, except for the money that would be raised by selling the furniture, the little bits of jewellery were all the children had. Having appointed himself guardian he had to do what he could to look after them. Allowing them their jewellery was hardly doing that.

'I am afraid, my boy, that would not be wise. I think it should be kept for you until you are out in the world.'

Peter shook his head.

'No, thank you, sir. We'll take it with us.'

Santa was amazed. It did not sound a bit like Peter talking. Such a grand, quiet, that-is-my-last-word-I-don't-want-to-be-argued-with kind of voice, just like a grown-up person.

Mrs Ford began to cry again.

'What a man he sounds. Brave little boy. When I first knew you, Peter, you were such a baby. Let them have their dear aunt's things, Mr Stibbings. It will be a comfort to them, poor pets.'

At the thought of how much the children would need comfort, Miss Fane clasped her hands and looked at the roof, and Madame Tranchot gave so deep a sigh that it nearly blew over a teacup. Mr Stibbings made up his mind.

'There are several little trinkets, dear boy, few of which would be any good to you. But there is a watch which you may have and Santa shall choose something as a keepsake. The rest I will deposit in my bank until you are older.'

Aunt Rebecca's jewel case had been locked in the corner cupboard when she died. Mr Stibbings had the key. He went now and unlocked it. While he was doing this Peter leaned down as if he had dropped something and whispered to Santa:

'Choose the one I tell you.'

During the last years of her life the duchess had made it a practice to give her faithful maid a piece of jewellery every Christmas. They were an odd-looking collection. There was the gold watch and chain for Peter. Aunt Rebecca had thought it very handsome, but she had never worn it because she was afraid of losing it. There were several heavy brooches, and there was one bracelet. It was plain gold, very dull and solid-looking.

Santa liked a brooch with turquoises, and hoped Peter remembered that she liked it. She had often said so when Aunt Rebecca wore it.

Peter fingered all the things in turn. He looked at Mr Stibbings.

'I don't suppose they are worth much, are they, sir?'

Mr Stibbings shook his head.

'In actual value, no. In sentiment, yes.'

Mrs Ford sniffed.

'Yes, indeed.'

'What I mean is,' Peter explained, 'if some day we wanted to sell them, would we get much money?'

'Sell them!' Mrs Ford's voice showed she was going to cry again.

'Well, we might have to. I mean, we might need the money for food.'

Mr Stibbings smiled.

'I hope not, dear boy. I think we can trust Saint Bernard's and Saint Winifred's to fit you for careers that will keep you from want.'

Peter nodded.

'Of course, sir. But I only said "supposing". You see, I want to know.'

Mr Stibbings looked vaguely at the jewels. But Madame Tranchot, who understood money, was turning them over.

'If it should be that you 'ad to sell them, Peter, it will be just the weight of the gold you would get. No more.'

'Well, Santa?' Mr Stibbings smiled at her. 'What do you choose?'

Santa looked at Peter.

'What would you have if you were me?'

Peter was still fingering the things. Suddenly he picked up the bracelet.

'This. You'll be less likely to lose it.'

Santa tried not to show what she felt, but the bracelet really was very ugly. She took it and held it out to Mr Stibbings.

'I'll have this.'

It seemed ages before bedtime, when Santa could be alone with Peter. Mr Stibbings stayed on and on in order to make last arrangements with Mrs Ford, and it was clear he would be there until quite late. But at half past eight Mrs Ford looked at the clock, and before she could say 'Bedtime' Santa had jumped up. Peter got up, too.

'I think I'll start my packing.'

Mrs Ford gave a knowing glance at Mr Stibbings as much as to say: 'Want to be together their last night, poor little things.' Then she kissed them both.

'Run along. Happy dreams.'

Peter and Santa went upstairs. At the top Peter said in a very loud voice:

'Goodnight, Santa.' He opened and banged shut her bedroom door. Then he opened his and dragged her inside. He shut the door and beckoned her over to the bed. They sat side by side and talked in whispers.

Santa began.

'Have you a plan?'

'Yes. We're going to run away.'

'Where to?'

'Our uncle. The one Aunt Rebecca had the card from every Christmas. We might stay with him.'

'We don't know where he is, and we haven't any money.'

'That's what the watch and bracelet are for. We'll sell them. And perhaps the card says where he is. I'll get it.'

Santa looked doubtful.

'Don't want them to hear you creeping about.'

Peter got up.

'They won't.'

Luckily the doorhandle turned very quietly. Peter stood in the passage and listened. Mr Stibbings and Mrs Ford were talking hard. Aunt Rebecca's room was at the end of the passage. Very quietly he opened the door. Would Mrs Ford have moved the card? He hoped not. Softly he crept across the room and felt round the mirror. There it was in the top left-hand corner. In a moment he had shut the door and was back in his room. Without a word he sat down beside Santa and they read the card.

It was a Christmas postcard with a picture of a church covered in snow on it. On the back it said:

> *Cob's Circus.*
>
> *Just a line, old dear, for the festive season. Hoping this finds you in the pink. Doing a four weeks' season with above and tenting with same April.*
>
> *Love,*
>
> *Gus.*

Peter and Santa stared at each other. They hardly knew what the word 'circus' meant. At some time or other they had seen a poster advertising one, and some vision of that had remained in the back of their heads.

'That's where people stand on horses,' Santa said.

'And a man sits on a lion,' Peter added.

Santa studied the card.

'Do you suppose our uncle's called Gus? What an awful name.'

'I don't see how it can be our uncle,' Peter objected. 'What would he be doing with a circus?'

Santa read what was written again.

'I wonder what "tenting" means. That's what he's doing now. It says April.'

Peter leant over her shoulder.

'So it does. I hadn't thought of that.' He got up. 'Look. Go to your room. Pack as little as you can in your case. Get into bed with all your things on except your shoes. Whatever you do, don't go to sleep. As soon as Mrs Ford's asleep, and she snores so loud I'll be sure to hear if I listen in the passage, I'll come and fetch you.'

Santa crept to the door.

'You'll bring my bracelet?' Peter nodded. 'Where'll we go to?'

He shrugged his shoulders.

'I don't know where we'll go tonight. Tomorrow we'll find Cob's Circus.'

12. Christmas Parties

*I*N LONDON *for many years we have been pitiably short of carol singers and bands which play carols. Maybe there are more in other parts of the country. When I was a child there seemed never a minute, in the evenings before Christmas, when some group was not on the doorstep singing 'Away in a Manger' or 'Good King Wenceslas'. Near the shops there were bands supposed to have come from Germany who played carol after carol to the great joy of the shoppers. Of course now there are loudspeakers in many shops blaring out carols, but to me loudspeakers have not the charm of live people.*

The high spot of our carolling came on Christmas Eve when the handbell ringers came to play carols to us. The handbell ringers played in the hall and everybody in the household sat on the stairs to listen. When it was over the players were served with mince pies and ginger wine. They left in a gust of 'Merry Christmas' and, as the front door closed on the last of them, one could feel the spirit of Christmas creep into the house. It was all done. The decorations were up, the tree was trimmed. Every present lay under it. In the kitchen the turkey was waiting for tomorrow and so was the plum pudding. Upstairs our stockings were ready to be hung up. It was a time to feel and just to soak in what Christmas meant.

In those faraway days, before we went to bed there was reading out loud of some Christmas story. Often Dickens's A Christmas Carol. *It is of course a terribly sentimental story, but I would swear there are few who by the end cannot hear the Christmas bells pealing and see the boy running to fetch the biggest turkey in the town.*

Lots of you have more than human beings to remember at Christmas. Presents are of course wanted for pets. I had a black miniature poodle

called Pierre, and I cannot tell you what Christmas presents meant to him. His, not so much prettily packed, as made difficult to open, were piled under the tree with everyone else's. In his were simple things like a little squeaky toy, a biscuit or a piece of cheese: he did not care what, his fun was to open his own parcels. Each time he was handed one he carried it to a corner of the room and only when he and everyone else had received all their presents would he unpack his. Then what an orgy of unpacking went on. Many people said watching Pierre and his parcels was one of the high spots of their Christmas Day.

I remember as clearly as if it happened yesterday my sisters and I being asked to a party. The card said '7–11 dancing'.

In those days many people gave dances, for all that was needed was to roll up a carpet and provide someone to play the piano. What was different was clothes. Today you go as you are, but in my childhood you wore a party dress. We were the daughters of a poor parson so we only had two party dresses each. Our best were white, so very much kept for best to keep them clean. Our second best were pink, of cheap material, and we hated them.

I cannot remember now why but my mother

had decided that party would be a second-best so we were sent wearing our pinks. Unknown to us the party givers were being visited by their only rich relations. Because of their arrival they had laid on the grandest party they ever gave. The carpets were not just rolled back, workmen had carted them away and polished the floors so they shone like a skating rink. The children of the house all had new frocks and so did those of their friends who were in the know. There was a buffet served by proper waiters. Every light in the house was turned on. But the final touch was a band. Truly only three-piece but renowned throughout the whole county and very expensive. Imagine the glory that we three saw and the shame of our second-best pinks.

I was never given to humility but I was near to feeling it that night and at last I could bear it no longer. Dragging my unwilling sisters with me I settled us down on the stairs where many of the rich relations of our host had parked themselves to eat some supper. I then began a loud cross-talk with my sisters (much to their embarrassment).

'If,' I said, 'we'd known it was going to be this sort of party we would have worn our blue silks *trimmed with sequins or our scarlet taffetas.'*

'Or our whites,' my eldest sister put in, struggling to get me back on to the path of truth.

By then I knew even our whites were unworthy of this party. My imagination ran riot.

'I'd rather have worn our gold. Everybody says how lovely we look in them.'

On I went, imagining a wardrobe fit for a princess. I did not stop until the rich relations had moved away back to the dance floor. Of course they hadn't believed us, why should they care what three shabby little girls in pink might have worn? But the fairy tale I had made up had done me good. I danced with my head high for the rest of the evening.

Extra!

Extra!

READ ALL ABOUT IT!

NOEL STREATFEILD

Christmas
with the
Chrystals

and other stories

1895 Born Mary Noel Streatfeild, 24 December, in Sussex

1902 Goes to school at Hastings and St Leonard's Ladies' College

1911 The Streatfeild family move to Eastbourne, and Noel goes to Laleham School

1913 Noel leaves school and enrols at the Eastbourne School of Domestic Economy

1915 Noel works as a volunteer in the kitchen of a hospital for wounded soldiers near Eastbourne Vicarage during the First World War and in 1916 moves to London to work in a munitions factory

1919 At the end of the war, Noel wins a place at the Academy of Dramatic Art (now called RADA) in London

1926 Begins a correspondence course for writing, and has a short story published in a magazine

1931   *Her first novel,* The Whicharts, *is published by J. M. Dent, and she is asked to write a children's story about the theatre*

1936   Ballet Shoes, *illustrated by her sister Ruth Gervis, is published by J. M. Dent, and it becomes an immediate bestseller*

1936   Ballet Shoes *is runner up for the first ever Carnegie Medal, awarded annually to a writer of an outstanding book for children*

1937   Tennis Shoes *is published. Noel travels with Bertram Mills Circus to research* Circus Shoes

1938   The Circus is Coming *is published, also as* Circus Shoes

1939   *Noel wins the Carnegie Medal for* Circus Shoes

1940–45   *Joins the Women's Voluntary Services during the Second World War and continues to write*

1944   Curtain Up *is published, also as* Theatre Shoes

1946   Party Frock *is published, also as* Party Shoes

1948   Ballet Shoes *is listed by the Library Association as one of a number of 'books which should always be in print'*

1949   The Painted Garden *is published, abridged and published in the US as* Movie Shoes

1951   White Boots *is published, also as* Skating Shoes

1954   The Bell Family *is published, also as* Family Shoes

1957 Wintle's Wonders *is published, also as* Dancing Shoes

1963 A Vicarage Family, *the first of her autobiographical works, is published*

1962 Apple Bough *is published, also as* Travelling Shoes

1975 Ballet Shoes *is adapted into a television series*

1983 *Noel Streatfeild is awarded an OBE*

1986 *Noel dies 11 September, aged 90*

1991 Ballet Shoes *wins the Library of Congress Children's Books of the Year award*

2007 Ballet Shoes *is adapted into a film starring Emma Watson, Yasmin Paige and Lucy Boynton as the sisters*

INTERESTING FACTS

Noel aspired to become an actress and spent ten years of her adult life training and travelling with various theatre companies.

Throughout her lifetime Noel wrote over eighty books and three autobiographical novels.

Noel claimed to have a 'blotting paper memory' to which she attributed her success in writing. She could recall with detail pets, holidays and Christmases from her childhood years.

GUESS WHO?

from

Christmas with
the Chrystals

A She had wonderful pearls round her neck and a magnificent emerald ring on her finger, and emeralds in her ears.

B 'He makes sandwiches of anything that's in the ice box; when there isn't much he makes do with bread.'

C . . . a tired young woman, with a face prematurely lined from standing too long hours in the store where she worked . . .

D On her head she wore a small black hat trimmed with a shiny buckle.

E She was small, thin, mouse-coloured all over, and nervous as a bird scared, though it is hungry, to pick up a crumb.

WORDS GLORIOUS WORDS!

Lots of words have several different meanings – here are a few you'll find in this Puffin book. Use a *dictionary* or look them up online to find other definitions.

Insolence – *rude and disrespectful behaviour*

Festooned – *to decorate something (such as a room) with chains, garlands or other decorations*

Enraptured – *receiving intense pleasure or joy*

Baize – *a coarse woollen material that is typically green and used to make aprons*

Exquisite – *extremely beautiful and delicate*

Commissionaire – *a uniformed door attendant at a hotel, theatre or other building*

IN
THIS YEAR

1959
Fact Pack

What else was happening in the world when this story was first published?

The Guggenheim Museum in New York City designed by Frank Lloyd Wright is completed.

The Barbie fashion doll is first released by the company Mattel.

Russia launches the spacecraft Luna 2, which crashes into the moon, becoming the first man-made object to reach the moon's surface.

The Disney film Sleeping Beauty is first released.

QUIZ

Thinking caps on –

Let's see how much you can remember from Christmas with the Chrystals! *Answers are at the bottom of the opposite page.*
(No peeking!)

1 **Where is Caldecote Castle?**

a) *Surrey*

b) *Hertfordshire*

c) *Kent*

d) *Dorset*

2 **What are the names of the three Cornelius children?**

a) *Paul, Julia and Romy*

b) *Patrick, Jessica and Reenie*

c) *Philip, Judy and Ruthie*

d) *Peter, Jane and Rinke*

How much money does Mrs Cornelius offer to pay Rosa and Ted?

a) *£50*

b) *£75*

c) *£100*

d) *£150*

What is Rosa's 'Mrs Beeton'?

a) *A cat*

b) *A cookery book*

c) *A gardening manual*

d) *An old friend*

What do the children sing around the Christmas tree?

a) *'Good King Wenceslas'*

b) *'Hark! The Herald Angels Sing'*

c) *'God Rest You Merry, Gentlemen'*

d) *'I Saw Three Ships'*

ANSWERS: 1) c 2) d 3) c 4) b 5) a

MAKE AND DO

Make your own Christmas angel window decoration!

Be creative and try out different colours and patterns to make a variety of angels.

YOU WILL NEED

* Coloured card
* Thread or wool
* Gold tissue paper
* Gold pen
* Tracing paper
* Gold pipe-cleaner
* Felt-tip pens
* Glue stick

1 Cut out a large heart-shape from your tracing paper to form the angel's wings and decorate with a gold pen.

2 Now cut out a large triangle from the gold tissue paper. Glue this on top of the tracing-paper wings to form the body of the angel.

3 Cut a circle out of the coloured card and glue it to the top point of the triangle, to make the head.

4 Now cut some strands of wool for the angel's hair and glue them on to the head.

5 Fold the gold pipe-cleaner in half and make a loop in the centre. Twist the two loose ends of the pipe cleaner together and stick this to the back of the angel's head to form a halo.

6 Finish your angel off by drawing on a face and adding any decorations you wish on to the body.

7 Finally, stick your completed angel on to a window and watch her sparkle!

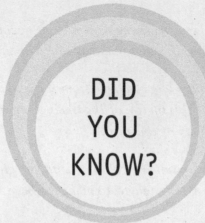

DID
YOU
KNOW?

All of the gifts listed in the 'Twelve Days of Christmas' song would equal 364 gifts in total.

Christmas trees are also known as Yule trees.

During the eighteenth century Christmas trees were traditionally decorated with candles, fruits and nuts.

Reindeer can run up to fifty miles per hour!

The all-time bestselling Christmas song is 'White Christmas' sung by Bing Crosby. It has sold more than fifty million copies around the world.

The world's biggest snowman was 34.4 metres tall and built in America.

Christmas pudding was first made as a form of thick soup with raisins and wine in it.

The Queen's Christmas Day speech was first televised in 1957.

PUFFIN
WRITING
TIPS

Watch the news and stay tuned to the latest happenings in the world – you never know what might inspire your next idea.

Read every draft out loud because it's the only way you'll find trouble spots – if you keep tripping up, think about how you could rewrite those parts.

Two heads are better than one! Find a writing buddy to test your ideas on.

If you have enjoyed *Christmas with the Chrystals* you may like to read *Christmas with the Savages*, written by Mary Clive, in which prim little Evelyn spends the Christmas holidays with the rumbustious, outrageous Savage children.

11. The Grotto

THE NEXT day Lionel was still angry with me. He refused to answer my well-meant remarks and became very affable to his own family. He even spoke to Betty, a thing I had never seen him do before.

The whole Savage family (except the baby) had become suddenly possessed with the idea that they must write a magazine. I expect actually it was Lionel who started the idea – he generally did start their ideas – but they all became keen on it and said 'magazine' over and over again as though it were some sort of password. Betty didn't know what a magazine was, but that didn't stop her from talking about it.

After breakfast the Savages all lay down on their fronts in a corner of the nursery and began to write. Betty could not write but she drew picture puzzles. The Glens, who did not like writing, went down to the still room to talk to Mrs Peabody.

I sauntered over to the group of Savages and stood beside them. None of them raised their heads.

'Shall I write something for your magazine?' I asked.

'No,' said Lionel, scribbling away hard. 'This is going to be a very unusual magazine and all the stories admitted to it are going to be good.'

'But I'd write a good story.'

'You couldn't.'

I returned sadly to the hearthrug where Tommy Howliboo was beating on an old tin with a stick.

'Why are you doing that, Tommy?'

'To keep away dwagons. Too many dwagons here.'

'Were you frightened of the dragons last night?'

'Course not. Me were only joking.'

He was a dear little boy when he was not frightened and I played with him for a bit, but I could not forget those older, bigger, more important children at the other end of the nursery, and I soon left him and went back to hover round the Savages. They still did not look up, but they made no objection to my reading the loose sheets of paper that were lying about on the floor; in fact Harry pushed a poem towards me with his foot. It was very short and went (I leave the spelling to your imagination):

> *Oh listen all ye Savages,*
> *About to choose a bride.*
> *Don't choose a one with asthma*
> *And don't choose a one that's died.*

Rosamund was writing a story called 'Nora's Adventure'. It was about a girl who was sent to school to improve her, and she got into the train at a small station in the north of Scotland. 'She sat sadly without looking up for a few minutes but as the whistle sounded something flashing in at the window attracted her attention. It was a splendid golden eagle. He caught Nora in his beak as the train began to move. Now although Nora was tall she was thin and light and so the eagle carried her quite easily. There was a strong wind blowing so neither the stationmaster nor the porter in the little Highland station heard her cries . . .'

'I'm sure the porter would have noticed,' I said, wishing to find fault.

'He might have on an ordinary day,' said Rosamund, 'but I've specially told you that a strong wind was blowing.'

'And also, if you said that Nora was small for her age it would be better.'

But Rosamund could not bring herself to make her heroine small for her age.

'No, it wouldn't. I've said she was thin and light and that's quite enough.'

I shrugged my shoulders, which was a gesture I was very fond of. I thought it grown-up but the Savages called it affected.

Lionel wrote so quickly that he had already covered many pages. His story was about school life and was called 'What happened to boys who committed murder and other bad things don't take their example'. In the preface he explained that 'the habits of the school are much like those of the school I am at', and as I had never been to school myself I read with interest to see what it was really like. Lionel's writing was terribly difficult, but as far as I could make out, school was a very tough place indeed. For instance, in the chapter called 'Trinity Sunday' they were all in the school chapel when there was a smashing of glass and a spear came flying through the window. 'It hit Ritard. With a cry he rose and walked out of the pew and fell dead in the aisle. The captain of the school carried him out and the service went on as if nothing had happened . . .'

Lionel, I knew, was not happy at school and really I was not at all surprised.

Writing stories looked so easy that I got some paper by tearing the flyleaves out of several books. To find a pencil with a point was harder, but fortunately I had had a diary in my stocking, so I took the pencil out of that and was soon scribbling away as fast as the others.

My story was about some children who had a shell grotto in their garden, and they dug up the floor of it and found some buried treasure underneath. So then they were immensely rich, much richer than any of the grown-ups, and they never had to do a thing they didn't like ever again. The buried treasure had been put there by smugglers, and that part I copycatted from a story about smugglers that was in a *Chatterbox Annual* which I had got for Christmas. *Chatterbox* had been kept in my bedroom and no one had read it except myself, so I knew that the others would not be able to catch me out.

But the others wouldn't even look at my story.

'We really don't want it, Evelyn,' said Rosamund, as kindly as she could, after whispering to Lionel, who said, not at all kindly:

'Take the bally thing away.'

I was disappointed and hurt. To make things worse, when the time came for me to go out for our morning walk I was slow getting ready and when I arrived downstairs I found that everyone was paired off and no one seemed to want me as a third, so that I felt more left out of it than ever.

I walked along the muddy road beside Marguerite who, as usual, was totally silent, and I brooded over my wrongs and over the beautiful buried treasure in the grotto which I had taken the trouble to invent but in which no one would take any interest.

I brooded all through rest and all through dinner, and after dinner when we were turned out into the garden, I said:

'Don't count me in the eena-meena. I'm not going to play. I'm going to see if I can't find this buried treasure.'

'What buried treasure?' asked Rosamund, falling into the trap.

'The buried treasure your grandmother was talking about,' I said.

'When was she talking about buried treasure?' asked Rosamund.

'I think I did hear her say something about buried treasure,' said Harry, unexpectedly coming to my help. Harry was so given to romancing himself that he really didn't know the difference between what really happened and what was just make-up. 'I wasn't supposed to be listening, but I do remember her saying, "Sure as eggs is eggs there's a blinking great packet."'

'I'm sure Grandmama never said anything of the sort,' said Rosamund. 'You've been reading something.'

'Didn't she?' said Harry. 'Oh, well, I remember now, what she said was, "The lucky beggar who finds it will get a tidy-sized 'oard."'

'Well, where did she say it was?' asked everybody.

'It was,' said Harry slowly, looking up at the sky. 'Let me see ...' His eyes wandered round searching for a likely place.

'I thought she said it was buried in the grotto,' I suggested softly.

'Yes,' said Harry. 'Grandmama, when she buried her buried treasure, did bury it in the grotto.'

'But that's ridiculous,' said Peggy, who was much the most sensible of the lot – in fact I might say the only sensible one of the lot, 'Grandmama wouldn't bury treasure. She can't dig for one thing.'

'Harry's got it a little wrong,' I said, 'the buried treasure has been in the grotto for ages and ages, only no one dares to dig it up because of the roof not being safe, and people only going into it occasionally.'

'But who put it there?' asked Peggy.

'Smugglers,' I replied at once.

'But there couldn't have been smugglers here. We're miles from the seaside,' said Lionel.

'That's why they came, of course,' I said. 'It was a safe place. The coastguards would look everywhere at the seaside but they wouldn't think of looking here.'

'True,' said Rosamund.

I could see that they were interested and, certain that none of them had read my *Chatterbox*, I went on, 'They were called the Nightriders because they rode by night. They had to get the treasure to London and, if you come to think of it, we are plumb in the way between London and the sea.'

After I had said this I wondered if I was right, but to my relief the older ones, who knew a little geography, agreed that this was so.

'Let's go and dig it up,' said Peter who, being young, thought things much easier than they are.

'We might at any rate go and inspect the grotto,' said Rosamund.

We went off to the corner of the garden where the grotto was. It looked very mysterious and a very suitable place for buried treasure, and even I began to think that there *might* be some there. Straggly laurel bushes cast a shadow over it, and the steps leading down to it glistened with damp.

Lionel descended the steps, unlocked the door and looked in. There were no windows, but a greenish light came through a ventilator in the roof, and when the door was wide open one could see all round the curious little place.

'I suppose it was the smugglers who brought all those shells with them,' said Rosamund, pressing close behind Lionel.

'Of course it was,' he answered. 'And now to find where the treasure is hidden.'

Christmas with the Savages
is available as A Puffin Book.